For
Jim
Peace &

1

Peace
INC.

— a novel —

Vijay Balakrishnan

Peacock  House

New York

Copyright © 2011 by Vijay Balakrishnan

Published in the United States by Peacock House™ LLC., New York

Library of Congress Number: 2011913094

ISBN 978-0-61-551695-0

graphic design by Charles Yuen

photos on front and back cover by Vijay Balakrishnan

Printed in the United States of America

peacockhousellc@gmail.com

for my family

...if not now, when?

Rabbi Hillel

table of contents

Don't misunderstand me. I'm as sickened as the rest. I lost a good month after the blasts with nothing going on but drinking and basic depression. Many of my so-called friends are also afraid, but me, I went past fear years ago when my world exploded in a blink. At the time, it didn't take a genius to figure out it was time to go, but I was still technically a kid, so I waited and patiently suffered until I could make my escape.

And where better than America, right? I scraped up enough for a plane ticket and a good lawyer. He did his job well, and presented, movingly I thought, what I would bring to the American mosaic. Why would the judge know a degree in English back home only means you're either too stupid or lazy to do anything useful? I was even allowed to make some closing remarks, and unfortunately I got carried away, concluding with "More than anything, your honor, I yearn to drink from the fount of freedom!" When it came out of my mouth I was definitely surprised and uncomfortable, and it was obvious everyone else was squirming too. Nonetheless, he gave me asylum.

What did I like best about America? Well, the most basic thing: self invention. And man, I was digging it. All those years of TV and rock and dissolute reading, all my wasted childhood fantasies were now indispensable. I changed my name and freed myself to maximize my opportunities in the land of milk and honey. For me, it is paradiso simply to walk in the produce section of my local supermarket. The abundance! It's dazzling, like heaven!

I am going into all this to make it clear how important it is for me to get on with life, even as I'm kept awake by the sound of ambulances and fire trucks, and every channel on TV is now the sci-fi channel, showing people in orange rubber suits spraying packages and envelopes with foam.

The night before the blasts, Elena and I were on the verge of calling it quits again. We'd been living together for six months, and after the first weeks of playing house, things quickly turned sour. Why? Naturally, there are always two sides in these situations, and I can only give you mine. The woman I believed was very much like me, ready for the big adventure, willing to make the most of this precious and all-too-quick existence, turned out to be as tedious as any other housewife. The transformation took me completely by surprise, as if overnight she became possessed by a particularly boring alien pod.

When I questioned her about the change, she treated me like I was the one betraying her. What happened to our dreams? I asked. To live with some imagination and intensity? At which point she would either do something violent (plate smashing, glass throwing, etc.), which I did not enjoy but could tolerate, or she'd cry in spasms for hours, which ended in me leaving the apartment until she calmed down. Once I stayed at my friend Milan's place, and when I came back the next morning, it was clear she'd cried the entire night. I said, Elena, this is not good, and I cannot accept this is in response to the dishes I was supposed to do when you were at work, but didn't get around to. I said it very sweetly, with obvious tenderness in my voice. I said, perhaps you should look into what has made you so unhappy, perhaps you should see someone professionally, perhaps there is some chemical imbalance. Instead of seeing my overt concern for what it was, she jumped up from the couch and rushed at me with her pretty hands bundled into fists. No, she didn't swing at me, though she did shove me so I banged against the wall. I realized the best response was not to react. She locked herself in the bathroom until the afternoon (I went to the café down the street to piss), and when she finally appeared and saw that not only had I done the enormous pile of dishes, but I'd even mopped the kitchen floor, she shed more tears, assuring me they were tears of joy and relief. We rode on the positive energy of that evening for another two weeks until the phone bill arrived and brought on another eruption.

In the following weeks, the conversation about breaking up fell into another sort of pattern, each time more definite, until the night before the blasts, it seemed like we had finally exhausted ourselves in every way. I'd called Milan and informed him that I would have to sleep on his floor until I could make other arrangements (it was Elena's lease), and I was sad about it all, but ready. Then the blasts.

Elena took it badly. Though she didn't know anyone personally, one of the hostesses who worked in her restaurant lost a husband, and though Elena wasn't particularly close to her either, she began to empathize with the woman's predicament until she made herself crazy with grief.

What could I do? Could I say to her, I am sorry, I agree this is a terrible tragedy, but I have already had my heart blown to smithereens? Could I tell her I was attempting to nurture a fresh heart, a new hope? Could I explain any of this and not appear either superior or callous? I didn't go to Milan's and instead stuck around to make sure she would be okay. And so far, it wasn't looking too promising. First, because of her condition, and the state of downtown, she skipped work as a hostess at Poncho through the entire second week, post-blasts. She assumed they were closed. Apparently they weren't. When he fired her, the manager said she shouldn't feel bad because they would have had to let her go anyway, business was terrible. So now she doesn't go anywhere and hangs around in her slip, chain-smoking American Spirits, watching the Terror Channel.

"Pumpkin," I say, cheerfully, "this will not do." I sip my espresso, waving the cigarette smoke out of my face. She is gazing into her coffee as if it were a crystal ball, tapping ash into the ashtray, her well-dyed chestnut hair falling over half her face.

"Whatever." Her favorite English word, the most annoying word in the language. She was already familiar with it as a teenager, long before she immigrated with her mother from Warsaw. She is susceptible to strong feelings and yet her speech can be post-interested. "What do you know?"

"Well, nothing extraordinary, I can assure you that much. What I do know is you should take a shower and get dressed. I'll take you to dinner and a movie. Dinner and a movie, sweetie!"

It almost works and she cracks a smile, the ripple lines forming in her cheeks, but just as quickly they vanish. Her face sobers. "Afternoon now."

"Lunch and a movie!"

This time I get no reaction at all. A few seconds later she lets out a tired sigh. "Do whatever it is you do. I do not need baby-sitter."

"Elena, please. Give me a break. Huh? Give me one fucking break."

She puffs her cigarette, and inhaling, winces in existential pain, before she juts her lower lip, blowing out a stream of smoke. Her eyebrows knit anxiously. "Look, I'm only saying, don't worry. I'll be fine."

"But you are distinctly not fine! You sleep fourteen, sixteen hours, you eat only shredded wheat and Skittles, you smoke two packs a day, you never leave the apartment..."

"I'm sorry I'm not strong as you, Bob."

Even after all these years it never fails to delight me when I hear my new name. It took weeks of list making and complex methods of evaluation to arrive at the perfect simplicity of Bob. And I insisted there be no other name, no middle initial, no surname, place name, or any other kind of affiliation. I wanted something as basic as possible on which to build my new life and Bob opened horizons. "It's not about that," I say.

I get up and go to her, gently massage her tight shoulders, kiss her head. From above I see her full breasts snug in her slip and I'm saddened the view arouses no passion. "You'll feel better. Promise."

She groans as I push on a particularly dense knot of muscle. "What part of whatever don't you understand?"

After the blasts there were many speculations about the status of irony. Which, excuse me, itself strikes me as ironic. What were these guys trying to say when they proclaimed irony is no longer possible? As if it rested on the absence of tragedy? Perhaps it is even the opposite, that saying the reverse of what you mean is a pre-emptive response to heartbreak. Can the weather be ironic? What a beautiful summer it was, and what a pristine morning was ruined that dark day. And now, what a perfect transition into autumn, the leaves, for a short week, yellow, orange, brown. Only the occasional breeze carrying the stink from downtown reminds you of the war, the ubiquitous war with no end in sight. There are days when the nip in the air and gentle sunshine under fluffy clouds feel like I'm being tested and mocked.

I get a take-out coffee and sit in the center of the park on a wide arc of benches facing two ancient trees. One trunk shoots straight up, its branches a generous canopy, the other tree twists away, boy tree and girl tree, moving apart from each other. It's brisk and sunny and the few people scattered around are a bit upscale, the newly unemployed, trying to sort it out. Behind me, on the lawn, the guy who looks like Hendrix (plays lefty and everything) is again rendering the

Star Spangled Banner, bombs, missiles and all. His amp isn't turned up too loud and the wind is blowing sound in the opposite direction, but the stray chord and the memory of Hendrix playing it, makes me feel desperate.

Yes, I must face facts. Elena is not working, and shows little promise of finding a job in the near future. She claims she will use the time to write her screenplay, which to me constitutes the opposite of a plan. I, unfortunately, have come to the end of any liquid reserves, my cards are nearly maxed, and my so-called business is held hostage by a maniac. Even if I manage to discipline Grace, who knows how the market for multi-culti greeting cards is affected by recent events? *Multi-Culti Cards, (registered trademark), For The New America. Full Range of Religious Holidays: Ramadan, Divali, Passover, Lent, Amitabah, Easter, etc., Plus, Classic Artwork (read public domain) From Around The World. All the standard holidays covered but with a fresh multi-culti twist!*

I finish my coffee, toss the cup in the garbage, and take the diagonal path. A man and a woman in green jumpsuits scatter leaves on the ground with tubes hooked up to noisy blowers. Some punky tattooed kids are passing a can in a brown paper bag. A red-faced Ukrainian drunk shouts obscenities at his equally pickled friend. Sparrows hop and fly, carefree.

I take the train to Milan's place. People still look worried, jittery. One burly guy has his jacket and scarf obscuring a small gas-mask. The train slows, then stops, starts again and stops, and against my better judgment, my heart races. I'm looking for exit doors, aware that I'd have no idea which way to run. I look to the burly guy as a detector or litmus, a psychic bomb-sniffer, more sensitive to threat than the rest of us. His head droops on his thick neck, his sausage fingers knit. Is he praying? The train picks up speed and I can feel our collective relief as the car pulls into the station and the doors open. I think of getting out, and walking... sixty blocks? I'm truly surprised to find myself rattled. I know a few things about fear, how if you take one step in its direction, through a curvature of emotion, you must take five steps back to find your way. I know how easily fear can rule your decisions, eat away your life.

I call Milan from a payphone and he comes down to let me in. His building is dilapidated, filled with Mexicans. At the back of the entryway, garbage piles up for no accountable reason, and jumbo rats frolic with abandon. Milan is unaffected by passing the infested corner, but I stamp and holler, making as much noise as possible. Two mid-size fellas scurry out from underneath a plastic bag, and as I flinch, I see they are trailed by a lumbering matted brown grandfather rat who stops to calmly watch us pass.

"This is a disgrace," I say. "Richest fucking country on earth."

"They have to live, too," Milan says in his irritatingly sagacious manner. I follow him up four flights to his apartment, and he points at one of the folding chairs at the kitchen table, which I occupy. "Coffee, if you like," he says. "Be right back. Devi has a little fever." He opens the door to the bedroom, and I hear Anna making baby-talk and little feverish Devi letting out one exhausted cry after another in a steady rhythm. Devi sounds like a dolphin. "Shhh, my princess," I hear Milan say, "shhhh."

I met Milan at an Entrepreneur Seminar many years ago. Fifty or sixty eager suckers expecting to learn the secrets of BIG BUCKS ON THE WEB for two hundred dollars. Who knows how many lives were ruined by the boundless enthusiasm of Jack, the twenty-three-year-old seminar leader? There were a few true-blue Americans there, but most were immigrants, looking for the big score. What I remember best from that wasted afternoon was how much the poor saps liked saying the kid's name. It buttressed their confidence in his useless advice, like the name could unlock the mysteries of American capitalism. So, Jack, you are saying I can make millions and I will never have to produce a thing? Fantastic! Jack, if I understand you correctly, there are people out there with millions they will give me for only my idea? Super! Jack, is it possible I can make millions and my company never has to turn a profit? Astounding!

"She's better." Milan smiles, shutting the door softly behind him. He pours himself a cup of coffee and sits down, his shoulder slashed by afternoon light. The light is the best aspect of Milan's tiny place, and he and Anna, though broke, give the apartment a romantic feeling of possibility, of beginnings. I know their life must be difficult but I've rarely heard Milan complain, which is certainly his best quality. "So?" he says, raising his brows, furrowing his high forehead. Every day he more resembles a Russian icon of a saint. If he had a beard he'd be a dead ringer for the Man himself.

"Grace is impossible," I say wearily.

Milan holds the cup with both hands as if he's warming them, lifts it up for a sip. "I talked to her yesterday."

"Oh? You didn't tell me that."

"Why should I have told you?" He deploys his placid stare, the lips ever so slightly turned up at the corners to suggest deep repose. Clearly, the conversation with Grace was about me, and it was unpleasant.

"No, that's not what I mean. I didn't mean that."

"You want to know whether we discussed you. Which is only natural. Of course, we did."

"I'm sure she made some wild accusations." I get up and go to the cabinet for a cup.

"No, in fact. She was calm. She says you owe her money."

"She's a criminal," I say, pouring my coffee. "She pretends she's such a mouse. Little Korean girl. So solly, so solly. Innocent child in the big bad city! Don't let it fool you, Milan. Sugar?"

"Second cabinet." His forehead rests on the tips of his fingers, his face lit up by a sunbeam. "She says different."

"Extortion!" I put in three spoons of sugar and stir. "We had a price, Milan! An agreed-upon amount!"

"Look, what's it to me, ultimately?" He shrugs and I'm annoyed, but of course, he's right.

I sit, trying to calm down. "Is it my fault what she's produced is worthless?"

"She claims you are the one who keeps changing his mind. She mentioned a "Remove Obstacles" card with the elephant-god Ganesh that she did twenty-two versions of."

"Yes! Because all twenty-two were wrong! Don't you see? This is for all the marbles, Milan! Every card must be perfect. We don't get another chance."

"You want to know what I think?" Milan often asked you whether you wanted his opinion, and it wasn't just a pose or rhetorical question. Once when he asked me, I replied, as calmly as possible, I wasn't interested, and he didn't even flinch before changing the subject. It was a quality I respected, yet there was a formality, a well-practiced aspect, that left me feeling odd. I mean, it implies our interaction is geared only to my benefit. By completely respecting my needs, he managed to have power over me. Every time he asked the question, and I said yes, I was humiliated. I feel diminished simply nodding.

"Bob, at this point, it doesn't matter who is justified. You have a situation. You can negotiate, maybe by offering some money..." I make a lemon-sucking face to show my displeasure for this option, "... or you can write it off as a loss and try again with someone else."

"Write it off? Milan, do I look like Microsoft to you? Fucking GE? I've already borrowed on my credit cards! That Mongol has ruined me. My only option is to threaten her."

"Small claims? Forget about it."

"Alright then, I'll phone incessantly. Stand outside her building. Follow her everywhere she goes. Glare at her. Order multiple pizzas. "

"She has cousins, Bob." I don't appreciate his smile. "Martial arts guys. I've met one of them. Built like a tank. He has his own Tae Kwon Do school."

Now I'm truly pissed. "That doesn't frighten me. Milan, you know me as a peaceful man..."

"Not totally."

"... but realize that I back away from nothing, from no one! Tae Kwon Do, my ass! I'll buy an Uzi!"

The door to the bedroom opens and Anna walks in, her forefinger raised to her puckered lips. "Shhhh. My God, what's happening out here?" Anna is half Indian and half German-Dutch, her skin is the color of milky cocoa, her eyes, nose and mouth are fine like a Persian miniature. She is slight, but sturdy with lovely, curvy, mommy hips. I could easily love her.

"Sorry, Anna." I hate to upset her. Whereas Milan's goodness seems to require cultivation, Anna is a natural. "Sorry."

Anna leans against the counter. "She's asleep," she says and Milan lifts his eyes to the heavens in thanks. "What's happened, Bob?"

"Some business troubles," I say.

"Things are tough, now. All over." Anna smiles, and it is clear I am to be reminded of the many thousands who died senselessly in our fair city, of the billions suffering needlessly everywhere, that I am supposed to put my petty struggles in perspective. It would take too long to explain that larger insanity does not make smaller insanity any less significant. You live where you live. A problem remains a problem. Bills must be paid, dammit! "How are you doing?" I ask her.

"All this is very hard with a baby. We talk about moving, but at least Milan has work here. We have health insurance..."

"The world is full of maniacs," I say.

"Not only," Milan says. "Most people want to live in peace."

These are the sorts of statements I find infuriating. Yes, most people want to live in peace, *on their own terms.* Is Milan so aggressively stupid? Let's only take the lovely twentieth century: WWI, 15 million; WWII, 50; Gulag, 15; China another 30; various revolutions, wars, tribal conflicts, maybe another 50 to 70, and that's just murder, those are just the sins of commission. For each person killed there is a killer, someone with the intent to kill, regardless of how they justify it. And for each person killed there is a mother, a father, perhaps a sister, a brother, a wife, a son, a daughter. Each killer has a reason, as reasonable or unreasonable as it might seem. And each killer also has a mother, a father, perhaps the rest. Most people want to live in peace. Did most people even live in peace when their circumstances were peaceful? Or did they go about creating mischief, tormenting their mate, their children, their community?

Milan began to make pronouncements of this nature starting about a year ago after he read a book by the Dalai Lama. I remember he took great pains to explain to me that he was not merely another victim of fashion, but in encountering "the teachings" and "the practice" he'd had a genuine epiphany. But like any person having gone through a religious conversion, he can be smug about his certainties. One ridiculous evening he spent hours trying to convince me I wasn't happy, that I would only be happy once I understood the nature of suffering and desire, and I, in equally ridiculous fashion, insisted on my well-being, and further insisted that desire was the thing that kept my happiness afloat. All in all, a complete waste of time.

"Anna, what do you think?" I ask. "With war and terrorism and the rest of it, do you feel there will be more or less of an interest in multi-culti greeting cards?"

She laughs. "Well, honestly? I'm not sure how many people will be buying greeting cards at all if they're out of money. And the multi-culti thing probably isn't as attractive after the attacks. You know, people close ranks. Maybe if you put an American flag on each one." Milan laughs, gets up and kisses her cheek. "Yes, Bob, that solves the whole problem. Simply make American flag cards." I'm not sure why he thinks this is so funny because he continues laughing as he rinses his cup and carefully places it in the dishrack.

"So, you think it's hopeless." I feel tremendous relief as the statement leaves my mouth. It was coiled inside for weeks, waiting to escape.

Anna gently punches my shoulder, comradely. "Come on, Bob. You're the one who used to give Milan pep talks in the old days."

Ah, the old days, before Milan met Anna, when he let me crash on his floor in the room where baby Devi is now peacefully resting. The old days, when Milan and I would spend endless hours at this very table hatching schemes to cash in on the biggest boom in history. But it took me time to learn the way things work here, to develop the necessary discipline, to understand that follow-through is everything. "Well, I guess I better be going," I say.

"Have some chicken curry," Anna says.

"Yes," Milan says. "Eat and go."

"No. Thank you. Thanks. I've got to figure out what to do." I get up and kiss Anna on the cheek. She smells of baby-powder and urine. I hug Milan.

"Peace," he says, winking, and I'm not sure whether I'm being lectured or provoked.

"Sure." I head down the steps, thudding my feet loudly to break up the rat party at the bottom of the stairs. "Most people want to live in peace." I mutter to myself, exiting the building. "What an asshole."

I pass a fruit-stand with a small American flag on a thin stick hanging limp on its corner, then a wrecked Mexican drunk wearing a flag bandana on his head, and then two stores and one taxi with flags plastered on their windows. Anna's right, of course, in a war, there's money in flags. But there's no room there: the network already in place, factories cranking out millions in China or Nicaragua or wherever. The largest markets are always cornered by the big guys. Most people want peace.

Then I start to wonder, just how many people? And would they pay?

CHAPTER II

Elena came out with it, the grievance behind all others, the molten core of her unhappiness with me. When we first met and I'd made it clear she'd have to take me as Bob, that I was unwilling to discuss my national origin, race, or religion, she not only tolerated it, but on numerous occasions proclaimed how interesting she found what she cutely termed my "universalness." It appealed to her political and spiritual idealism. For many months in the first blush of our romance my so-called past was a source of great fun as I would make up various histories (Turk, Greek, Tajik, Albanian, Venezuelan, Kashmiri, Muslim, Catholic, Jew, Hindu, and other cross-pollinations of parents and heritage) and she would try to expose the lie. It was hot! I wasn't foolish enough to expect we would continue the game indefinitely, but I did think that Elena understood I was serious. Yet, slowly the game grew ugly; she insisted, pleaded, demanded, I tell the truth.

I explained that to get on with life, I knew (regardless of what anyone else felt) my so-called past was better jettisoned into oblivion. It was nothing but gravity and pain and haunting. Not to mention the worst of it, nostalgia. I wanted, like religious physicists and highly evolved yogis, to live in the moment. Brutal and random destruction reminded me how important it is to be in the *now*.

Yes, I enumerated all these points to Elena, to no avail. She claimed my behavior was psychotic, or at least, she conceded, borderline. Bringing all her pop-therapeutic acumen to bear, she thought I had not grieved sufficiently, and instead I'd had a psychotic episode, attempting the annihilation of my identity and memory. And I said, yes! Absolutely! It is a kind of self-annihilation; a process, if followed purely, takes you beyond the heavens, say the mystics. Bob was my first step. Perhaps Bob will be the last step. I cannot make Elena understand the full scope of her demand. What she sees as merely a question of emotional intimacy threatens my very psychic survival. Bob cannot look back. There really is no back to Bob.

"This is exactly the kind of bullshit I'm talking about," Elena says. We are taking a stroll through the lush park (Elena's idea, the only thing that would get her out of the house). We thought of going to the museum to see Brueghel drawings but the lines came spilling out the doors as each person was searched for bombs. Soldiers in camouflage and helmets were leading German Shepherds up the museum steps. So we walk to the park, and Elena uses the calm to make her case again, as though the golden autumn, rosy children, and bounding dogs will soften my resolve. "You are creating an entire justification for not dealing with your feelings. It's so damn obvious."

"I'm choosing what I want, Elena. To live every moment as unencumbered as possible. And I'm managing it. Not perfectly of course, but I'm generally optimistic, understand? That's who Bob is. Me. " I stop her and we turn to each other; I cup her luminous face in my hands, she closes her eyes. "Elena, I adore you." I'm not sure why I say this, although it is true in a way. I kiss her lips softly.

"Such crap," she says, pulling back. Her pace is brisk now. I struggle to keep up, the leaves crunching loudly under our feet. "Put yourself in my shoes. I... I... I opened up to you. I told you my childhood, my dreams. I wanted to share my life with you." She is sniffing now and I hate it that I feel only annoyance. "I don't even know what you are!" She cries out, her sweet voice breaking down into sobs.

"Please." I grab her arm, and hold her firmly by the shoulders, thrilled by her fine muscles. "You know exactly what I am!" I kiss her with all the gusto I can manage, trying to reanimate the memory of our early lust. Her lips stay sealed and she pushes me away. I notice she doesn't have her smell, the chemical attractors, elective affinities, disconnected. "Pumpkin," I say, reaching out.

"How am I supposed to trust you?" she asks, pushing my hand away. "You might be a murderer. Or, or, a terrorist, for that matter. You've got the looks."

My silence clearly conveys I am hurt by what she says. She knows I didn't lie to her about my so-called past, and now she feels guilty for her provocation. "I understand you're upset, Elena. Can we sit somewhere?"

In one fluent movement, she sits down on the carpet of red and orange leaves. I join her, the grass damp and cold. "We're sitting," she says. Her mouth is slightly downturned. I wish she would take off her sunglasses.

"I spent years a wreck, you know that" I say, staring at the bright green veins of an orange maple leaf. "I've told you some things. I did see... various doctors, psychiatrists... I took all kinds of medications. I mourned, I cried, I went numb...sure. All of it. Then I too had to die. You see? That guy had had it. He was done. Kaput. In anguish one moment and the next I felt so light, so free, at peace. He took his pain with him, and I must leave it alone. I realize it is asking something special from you. But I have never been unclear about my heart, and you can feel it, Elena." I pick up the maple leaf and hand it to her. She tears at the edges of it, quiet for a long minute.

"I was talking with Jackie about this," she says, "and she was shocked."

"Jackie. Big deal."

"No, Bob, she was disgusted you would maintain the secrecy with me."

"You still don't understand! It is not a secret. It has been banished, cast out. There is no there there any longer. And I go looking for it at my own peril... What else did the ever-insightful Jackie have to say?"

"She says you need therapy."

"Pah. Who doesn't?"

"You more than some others."

"Elena, what do you most like about me?"

"At the moment, not very much."

"No. Even right now. If you had to pick one thing."

"You're cheerful, I suppose."

"Exactly! Therapy can't even promise me that much."

"You're happy?"

"More than most."

"This is an obnoxious attitude, Bob."

"I made real sacrifices for it. I paid with my past. I'm not sure how many people would."

"Even more obnoxious." She crumples the leaf and tosses it at my face. "Don't you see? You're not blending in at all. If you wanted to blend in, you would have a last name, a place of birth, a religion, a history, a..."

"Family?"

"Bullshit, Bob. We're not doubting your pain. Only your response to it."

"The royal we, eh? The ones who sit in judgment of a happy man. Besides, who the hell wants to blend in?"

She takes off her sunglasses and lies back, her clasped hands a pillow. She squints at the open blue sky, then shuts her eyes, relaxing the muscles in her face until she reaches angelic tranquility. Her rough suede jacket is open and her breasts stand proud under her favorite black beatnik sweater. Her matching suede skirt is hiked up to the middle of her thighs, her thin legs in gray tights and zip-up knee-high boots completing the Paris '68 dreamgirl. I am pulled to her, I don't even think of resisting. I can almost see attractor molecules forming in the air, a seamless chain from her knee cap to my eye. As I near, smell attractors are also active, linked, and I wonder whether it is only in my imagination, or as in the past, a shared event. I kiss her cheek like a schoolboy trembling with anticipation, with hunger. Her lips look juicy like summer plums. "Lovely," I whisper.

Elena inhales a deep breath and holds it for a few seconds before flaring her nostrils to let the air escape. "The sad part is you've been nicer to me than anyone else. It's true." Her voice is saturated with resignation worthy of a Polish grandma. And although the admission is both self-dramatizing and pathetic, and ought to be an instant turn-off, chemicals have begun to override any interpreting. I wrap my hands around her waist, pulling close. She opens her sky-blue eyes and I cannot stop my spirit from diving in. We have been here before, the electricity familiar. We kiss, tongues twine, and we know we are again blessed and cursed. She's heated up, trembling, face flushed. I slide my hand under the elastic of her tights, caress her smooth bottom, and gently my fingers reach for her spot. And what is truly fun about Elena is that when she's in the mood, just my touch gets her off.

"Peace?" Elena says and bursts out laughing. We are cocooned back at home in a post-coital bubble, so her laugh is not derisive, although it teeters on the edge. "This is your big plan? The big secret?" She rolls over, straddling my leg, kissing and licking my neck, trying to get me up for another round. "Fantastic," she whispers, lascivious and wet, into my ear. All of which would have been more than acceptable under normal circumstances, but now I'm irked because I don't get the feeling she appreciates my genius.

"Yes, peace," I say, peevishly. My hands on her butt-cheeks are clearly signaling her to stop gyrating. She does, the torque releasing through her torso and into her neck, head swiveling to the opposite side of mine, where she starts working my other ear with breathy whispers. "Peace," she rasps so sexily that even against my wishes I feel a boner forming. I gently pull away, insinuating her onto her back. I sit up, putting my arm around her, in a loving, no-sex-right-now way. She rests her head against my chest, pouting with seductive petulance. "Look," I say, "since the dawn of history there has been war. You could say, in fact, history is the justification of war. A struggle for resources from the very start. One empire, ruler, conqueror, after another. And yet if you asked most people at any time what they valued, peace would be a basic requisite. Elena?"

"Yes, go on," she says, drowsily. "I'm listening."

"So, from the beginning of recorded time, the spoils of war have been trumpeted. But who, in the meantime, was making money on peace? See, it is a polar and necessary drive, Elena, the drive to harmony. So who has cashed in on that? Aha!" I free my arm from beneath her shoulder and she jerks awake. "Jesus! What? What happened?" Her face shows the stress of the rudely awakened. "I was listening." She leans her pillow against the headboard, sitting up, crossing her arms across her breasts.

"Who cashed in?"

"I'm supposed to know? You're asking me?"

"Who? Churches, of course! Religion in all its stripes! Peace in this world, afterworld, this life, next life, whatever. So peace came with the full package, including a God of some sort, and mediators to us mere mortals, a clergy, rituals, etc. And of course, history shows this was quite a lucrative business, soul-tending. In fact what you are 'buying,'" I make the scratch marks in the air, "is peace, and you are persuaded to buy the full package. See?"

"No."

"I read an article about New Religious Movements. They call them NRMs. And the market is booming! All kinds of wacky combinations! People are signing up by the millions!"

"I read the very same article, Bob. It said most NRMs fail miserably."

I leap out of bed, slip on my boxers, and pace. Elena lights a cigarette. "Yes, they fail, because they haven't properly defined their market niche. I have given this considerable thought, Elena. I don't want to start a religion. Too difficult. Too many loonies. Too much overhead. Not to mention messing with God, which why risk? But what if I can create a place for people, a set of symbols, a lifestyle, a website, which connects them to others who wish the most basic thing in life: to live in peace."

"It's idiotic. And I still have no idea what it is you want to do."

"Peace has never been properly marketed."

Elena chuckles, and its dismissive edge signals we have definitely left our post-coital haven. "It has never been marketed because it is not a thing, Bob. You can't market an idea, a, a condition."

I wait a few seconds, pretending this has not occurred to me. "Freedom? Equality? Justice? Science? Reason? Democracy? Fascism? Communism? Capitalism? Nationalism? God? None of those are *things* and they've been marketed pretty damn well! But peace? Aside from the religions, who? Gandhi is about it. MLK. A few ineffectual pacifist groups."

"Sixties? Seventies? John and Yoko?"

"Sure, sure. And we can use all that stuff for marketing."

"What is it exactly you sell?" Her tone is all business.

"Well, that... I haven't decided yet."

Elena laughs, coughing smoke, stubbing out her cigarette. Coughing and laughing, she goes to the bathroom, and pours herself a glass of water. She takes a sip, leaning against the doorjamb. Her smile is indulgent, cheeks pink, her pretty body in the late afternoon light, girlish like a Degas dancer. "Did I ever tell you about the man on the train?" she asks.

"No. I don't think so."

She walks over to the bed, setting the glass on the night table. She lies down on her stomach, arms at her sides, legs slightly apart. Her face is half lost in the fluffy pillow and yet her eyes are looking up at me.

"When I was young girl, I was travelling with my mother from Krakow to Warsaw, and this strange man entered the compartment. He rode with us for a few hours, twitching nervously, looking at us, then looking away, frightened almost. He was very thin, with a sparrow's head and a small gray mustache. I liked him immediately because what my mother worried was insanity was to me like a living cartoon. Eventually, he introduced himself and it seemed to calm him down. He told us he was going to Warsaw to get patent on a machine. And then looking around the empty cabin to check if anyone was listening, he told us excitedly it was a perpetual motion machine. I was thrilled by this, and began to ask questions, even though my mother kept pinching me, and I didn't understand why. He went on about the mechanics, the solar component, the chemical reactions, and I listened spellbound, as my mother was growing angrier all the time. Finally, my mother said, and it impressed me a lot, 'It sounds like the entire process depends on the first catalyst to start the machine.' And the man looked shattered as he nodded yes. 'And it sounds like you have no idea whatsoever what that catalyst is,' my mother said. The man, completely destroyed, shook his head no. He was quiet all the way to Warsaw. Years later, out of the blue, my mother said she regretted what she did to that man."

I kiss her shoulders, small kisses down the center of her back. "You think I'm like that man?"

"I... don't... want... to... be... the... one... to... find... ou... ou... oo... oooo..."

I left Elena working on her script. She claims to spend as much as ten hours a day at it. I have witnessed her sitting for eons staring into the screen of her laptop. Eventually, she said my very presence, anywhere in the vicinity (even if I went to the living room and shut the door) somehow thwarted her creative energies. I can understand it. I may not be an artist in her sense, but I like to think I am sensitive to art, to the art of business at least (even if my results so far have been dubious). I understand how in certain states you can be too sensitive to brainwaves in the ether. So, we try to work out times when I'll be gone, or she'll go to the café to write. I've asked what the script is about but she guards it like a secret spell. If she talks about it, she says, she won't actually do it, or she could jinx it. I understand that too, though I must admit it hurts a little she doesn't trust me. And then I think, maybe this is her unconscious way of taking revenge.

I know she is capable of cruelty. I have, shamefully, taken pleasure in it in the past. When we first met, she was basically living with a man. I'd gone to Xeno, the airport lounge bar downtown, where my friend Iqbal is a bartender, and at some point when Elena came to the bar to buy a round, Iqbal introduced us. I was smitten the instant I saw her, before I noticed she was returning with drinks to her obvious mate, a plain-looking blond corporate type, and another friend, who at the time I thought was super-foxy and who has since mutated into the ever-irritating Jackie. Anyway, her beau seemed almost uncomfortable handling the social responsibility of escorting two such hotties. He was tucked into his chair and kept scanning the room for predatory interest from other males, of which there was a truly palpable dose. One rasta-stud walked up and slouched into his routine, and was coolly rebuffed. A few of the leering men took this as a signal to forget it. What can I say? I was feeling good. And I was already introduced. And Iqbal had been complaining about his life as an aspiring DJ for what felt like hours. I walked over decisively, noting that the beau (I think his name was Rich) very casually placed his hand on Elena's thigh. *Back off! Mine! Grrrr!* He made sure he was talking to Jackie when I got there, so I'd have to wait to introduce myself.

That little maneuver cost him greatly in the end, because he freed Elena for the one crucial instant when our eyes met. The hand on her thigh was for my benefit, not hers. He should have been looking at *her*. I think he lost her right then. The rest of the evening could be seen as cruel from a certain perspective (his). Elena and I started talking in a code we freely invented as we went along. And the code wasn't even in language—we kept up what amounted to a banal conversation—but in pauses, inflections, baseless laughter. We both knew we were tormenting poor Rich, and it fueled our erotic yearnings. The first few months we were together she was technically with him. She got him to buy her things till the very end and left him with the confirmed belief it was his fault. I know all this because I was there, and though I found aspects of her contempt for him contemptible, she did leave him for me, so I can't complain. She said at the time he'd lost all his mystery. I wonder if she remembers that.

Well, for the moment she is happy, which is the important thing. I cannot have turbulence in the house when I am trying to gestate something so major. Elena need not be convinced of the brilliance of my plan as long as she doesn't actively sabotage it. So, I'm in fact sufficiently calm, well-oiled, and composed enough to meet with Grace. I suggested coming to her apartment/studio, but she said, in a way I couldn't exactly interpret, that she would rather meet in a public place, as if she worried for her safety with me. And here I was trying to make a peace offering, literally (and also, of course, from a business point-of-view). She agreed to meet me at Xeno, although I don't think she knew it was a bar. I decide to get there early, hit Iqbal up for a Ketel One martini, and mull over my pitch.

The walk down the avenue is melancholy. Funny how quickly things transform. I remember it first as a scary strip of junkies and bums; then in a few years it morphed into a boulevard of hair-stylists and bistros, sidewalks jammed summer nights with pretty young things waiting for tables. Now it is suddenly desolate again, and in the hours I spent indoors, the day became night and autumn tipped into winter: I can see puffs of breath. It's peak time on a Thursday night and the cafés are empty, bistros merely sprinkled, and the faces peering into their wine glasses look scared. A pair of bundled-up kids laugh, rough-house on the corner, but every passer-by seems inward, defensive, alert to the distant sirens of ambulances.

At least there's a cutie outside Xeno talking on her cellphone, frantically puffing a cigarette. "You're a dick! Oh, I can't believe it! No! Jerko!" she shouts as I push the glass door open and go in. They took great care designing the place, no question. One's only complaint is it might be overdone. The space-age steel and glass bar as you walk in and the 50s airport-lounge in the main room, the trippy tunes, all the details just so. I see the top of Iqbal's shiny black hair as he sits crouched taking inventory.

"Assalamualaikum my brother," I say.

Iqbal looks up grinning. He marks something on a piece of paper, then gets up to present his fist. We knock knuckles.

"Sup, bro," Iqbal says. He grew up around the corner and he's certainly not orthodox, although I know he secretly disapproves of drinking, especially women drinking. This prejudice, however, hasn't prevented Iqbal from taking advantage of certain drunken women, who come regularly to moon over his subtly unibrow handsome face.

The liaisons, albeit few and far between, left him disgusted and guilt-ridden. Ever since he hooked up with Farah, his new Bangla girlfriend, the "Women for Iqbal," as I call them, still frequent the bar, and poor Iqbal has to be nice to them for his tips.

"What news of the Women for Iqbal?" I ask.

"Why you do that, man? I'm making you a martini, and you giving me shit." He shakes the silver tumbler, carefully drains out a beauty, plopping two olives in it, and slides the glass towards me. I take a slurp off the top.

"Women for Iqbal?" he asks with a shy, self-important smile. Now that he's settled down, he loves being teased about it. He's still pretty young and enjoys the mythology of his power, in whatever form. "They come around." He leans on the bar. "They tip big."

"I bet they do," I say in a queeny tone of voice. "Big, mm-hmm." I look him up and down like I'm a buyer.

"Sick," he says but he is clearly happy for the attention.

"Let me ask you something." I sip my fine drink. "What do you think of peace?"

"Like piece of something?"

"I meant peace, like living in peace."

"Yeah. So, no war."

"Yes, that's what I meant."

"Yo..." shaking his head, "that's some heavy shit, man. Peace? I been thinking about it a lot, actually. You know, we had all the memorials and stuff..."

"Yeah?"

"I don't talk about it, you know? Everything's so fucked up. You have a lot of things to be pissed off about.

You know? So, I don't talk about it, but I think about it. And you know what I kept thinking about more and more? About those guys. The suicide guys. Crazy, man, I couldn't get them out of my head. These guys got nothing to lose. As to why that is, everyone has a different idea, but the fact, you know? See, I got all kinds of things to lose. Like peace of mind, for example. Yeah, peace." He gets a tall glass, fills it with ice and seltzer. He sips, gazing into nowhere.

"Not so warm and fuzzy?"

He laughs. "Definitely not. I'd like to kick someone's ass," he says, distracted. Two semi-cuties are at the bar tittering before settling on Cosmos. As Iqbal turns to make the drinks, they bump into each other with a suppressed twitter. Iqbal is having his usual effect on the ladies. The boy is blessed, I tell you.

I check my watch. I still have a few minutes for prep before she arrives. I don't have any kind of fixed routine, but over time I've determined there are a few things which are very helpful to do before making any kind of pitch. The object, immediately before the performance, is not to remember the material (by now, you should have insured it is second nature), but to forget it completely. Like any performance, at the moment you're *on*, you can't be thinking too much, you can't be consumed by what you're *supposed* to do. So one trick I learned from Stanislavski, who I think copped it from Gurdjieff (a genius of a salesman): Go into the corner and don't think about a monkey for one minute. Well, try it... You see the conundrum. I focus on my hands and feet, and fortunately one can stretch them in public without notice. Loosen the fingers, the toes, gently massage the palm, rotate the ankle... "Bob?"

Rats! She's early. I turn, composing myself for Grace's diminutive manipulation, her passive-aggressive poker face. I know I should be bright and confident, not in the least defensive. And the smile must not be exaggerated... I turn and find myself facing the formidable square head of a Korean man (I assume he's Korean, since he's with Grace— at close range I really wouldn't know). "Bob," she says as the stare-off with the man becomes uneasy, "This is my cousin, Tommy. Tommy, Bob."

"Pleased to meet you." I put out my hand. He waits a second or two, holding the stare, Bruce Lee-style, then crushes my hand in a kung-fu vice-grip. No doubt he is the Tae Kwon Do master Milan mentioned. Point taken. He releases my mangled paw, smiling ever-so-slightly to let me know he means business too. "Yeah," he says.

I make no secret of trying to wiggle my fingers back to life. "Nice to see you, Grace. Would either of you like a drink?"

"No," says Tommy. Grace is staring at the ground.

"Okay," I say. "Let's sit down." I lead the way up the transparent Jetsons steps and into the lounge proper. Since it's still early for Xeno, we find an empty table in the corner. Tommy pulls his chair close to Grace. I sit facing them. "So..." I say. "Here we are." *Quicksand, Bob, quicksand! This guy's spooked you already! You're lame, son! Garbage! You're nothing! Nothing!* "Grace, I've come with a proposal," I say, my voice pretty steady.

"What?" says Tommy.

"I don't understand. Are you her representation? Grace?"

She's unresponsive, shamelessly doing her inscrutable routine. "Yeah," says Tommy, "Consigliere." Again, the I-can-have-you-for-a-pre-breakfast-snack smile. "Like in *Godfather*. What's the proposal?"

"Come on, Grace," I say. "We can talk to each other. We don't need this."

"You owe me money, Bob," she says flatly. I got to her... a little at least. She spoke.

"Two grand," says Tommy.

A heartbeat before taking the big plunge. It's the best and worst moment: when there's no turning back. "Yes, you're right," I say, and it is the first time I've made a clear admission of the debt. "I thought about what you said, about your hours, and my... er... perfectionism. I see it from your side. Your time is money. You work for a salary. Yes. I owe you two grand."

Tommy, showing little finesse in these matters, cannot hide his surprise at the early victory. He's completely thrown off, since he was winding up to break me down in some way. Tommy looks to Grace for direction. "Good," she says. "I'm glad we agree about that." Not a flicker from her, the little Mata Hari.

"So, there's a few ways to work this out," I say.

I feel Tommy's tremor as he re-locates his purpose here. "Wait." Hand up, palm in my face, Northern Yunan Style. "One way. You pay."

"Yes, Tommy. That is one way. Look," I say and my tone is resigned, tired. "Just hear me out. Okay?"

Grace thankfully lowers Tommy's hand. Tommy keeps me fixed in his ass-kicking stare. "Thanks. Grace, what I have to offer is a percentage."

Tommy bursts out laughing. He's really turning into a problem. "Percentage? Of what? Any percent of zero is zero."

"Bob, I am not interested in a percentage of Multi-Culti Cards," says Grace.

"Fine. I'm not talking about those cards. I'm talking about something truly exciting, a real breakthrough in fact, like finding oil in the ground."

"Oh brother," says Tommy.

"More than anything, people everywhere want to live in peace, right? No one wants to be molested, shot, tortured, destroyed. Not one sane person wants that. So, we all agree about that, right?"

"Cut to the chase," Tommy says.

"Nobody has really marketed peace."

"You watch the news?" Tommy says, "Look around? People want to rumble. Someone attacks you, you don't turn the other cheek. Not in real life. You do, you keep getting smacked... Somebody's got to pay for this. What are you talking about?"

"Yes, all true. Attacks, counter-attacks, wars, bloodshed, empires, collapses, it goes on and on. Tommy, listen to me, for a second. Grace, please. Think bigger. You look around, in some way every belief promises peace. Even the most insane generals want their own countries to be at peace. Their own families. See? Very obvious. And so it is taken for granted, until it is threatened. Nobody wants to spend their lives waiting for the next calamity. So, if we are afraid now, there is also a part of us that yearns to explore peace, be at peace. People talking across borders, religions, ethnicities, ideologies! If only to know your supposed enemy also only wants peace!"

"Fuck that," says the resolute Tommy, "Two grand."

"What is your plan, Bob?" asks Grace.

Hot-doggy! "Look, I have to work it out. But what I'm proposing is the two grand converts into your initial investment in the company, Peace INC., and for that you'll own twenty percent."

"Of what? Of what?" says Tommy, and I'm happy to notice he also addresses Grace. He too can sense she's left an opening.

My speech speeds up a notch. "We start with a new logo or set of logos. Trademark a T-shirt or some products, like condoms, you know, "Make Love Not War," cute stuff. But the way to kick it off is a catalog and website. You do web stuff, right?" I say to Grace, as though we're already working together. She doesn't nod, but I'm sure she blinks assent. "So, my thought is a creative website and catalog of products that we order in small units as we get orders. The website we promote through every channel worldwide interested in peace, peaceful solutions, peace groups, activists, priests, yogis, students, anybody. Major portal. We place a few quirky pieces in some magazines, whatever. And... see where it goes."

"You're nuts," says Tommy.

"Maybe. It all depends on what we come up with. How imaginative we can be. What do you say, Grace?"

She hasn't spoken for awhile. She sits staring into her lap.

"Two grand. Cash," says Tommy, softly banging the table with his knuckles.

"Grace?"

She looks up, blank as Hello Kitty. "Fifty percent."

CHAPTER III

Hooray for the New Delaware Gap Bank! They were the only one out of twenty-two who issued me a card, with a five thousand dollar cash advance, which I promptly took. Peace INC. was launched! At least in theory. What followed was a gruesome month of Grace and me sitting in front of her giant Macintosh screen, trying to dream up a company, a logo, a new peace sign, any peace-related products.

Grace would barely speak, though she'd have a variety of designs and graphic possibilities up on the monitor. I have to admit I was impressed by the amount of thought and work she'd poured into our venture. She'd invented some clever standard variations, a 3-D model, one with the earth, the globe, the solar system, the galaxy, abstracted doves in Escher shapes, all beautifully done. We started off well, everything was going smoothly, until I began to ask questions about using any reference to the old peace symbols at all. Grace stared at me for a quiet minute, then said our meeting was over. When I said I didn't mean to upset her, she replied she merely had a headache. The next day we had a high old time brainstorming a peace mascot: Mr. Peace (too sexist),

Ms. Peace (too gendered), Dr. Peace (too prescriptive and a bit sinister), Plain Peace (an androgynous green smurf—just too stupid), Peace the Dog (the front runner! He wears a red bandana!) etc. We were desperately lost.

Then came a truly dark patch when we tried to nail down our "brand concept" in a phrase. Nothing is as nightmarish as stuck ideas, except sharing them. Our best effort after three long hellish sessions: "Wars Come and Go. Peace is Forever."

By then I was so disgusted I'd tricked myself into a fake epiphany. It was only when I reached home and, giddy, announced to Elena that we'd had a breakthrough, that I heard my growing desperation. Elena was nice enough; she fixed a cleansing bitter salad and squash soup and put me to bed. She's been very kind to me recently, though not very passionate.

So, Peace INC. was dead in the proverbial water. Couldn't lift off. Couldn't even take the first baby step. Grace and I decided to stop meeting for awhile, hoping the separation might inspire new thoughts. I spent the weeks drawing signs, symbols, diagrams, conjuring up marketing strategies, expanding the idea of the website to include Peace Rooms, Peace Links, Peace Products, Peace Diets.… Elena and I alternated days in the apartment to work, and though I kept busy and filled much paper, I knew I wasn't seeing it yet. My despair was further attenuated by Elena giving me reports from the Terror Channel (she'd cut down to an hour long check-in at night) about the progress of the Never Ending War. You see, I didn't want to know. I'd stopped reading the paper, stopped watching TV, stopped following it, because I didn't want to be distracted, discouraged. But Elena kept me posted on the victories, the success of the micro and macro bombing techniques, the relative order restored and disturbed again with relatively few casualties (by world historical standards).

Yes, of course I am glad for the relative peace inside America (by world historical standards). But the economy is definitely tanking, and folks seem to be channeling their fear into a variety of crypto-fascisms. Not good for Peace INC. No es bueno para mi. I realize with some nausea the cynicism of my premise: for the foreseeable future the species will not escape bloodshed. Brooding endlessly on how to tap into the other side of animal fear, and getting nowhere, despondent, I reach for the phone just as it rings.

"Bob?"

"Grace, I was just about to call you."

"Yes, yes, I'm sure you were." It sounds like she's crying. "Are you okay?"

"Okay?" Now I realize she's laughing. "Okay, yes! Very okay. Very very okay. It happened, Bob. The miracle, it happened."

She wouldn't explain further, so I rush over and, uncharacteristically, loud music (sounds like N Sync) blares from inside. I knock forcefully, the music shuts off, and an ebullient Grace answers the door. Her hair is pulled back, making her face less round, her cheeks are rosy, her smile pretty. She's beaming, taking my arm (which I find peculiar—we never break the personal space bubble), and leading me to the computer. "See," says Grace.

On the screen against a pale electric-blue background floats a golden traditional peace sign, but it doesn't stay still, revolving on one axis, then another, tilting from one angle to the next, speeding up until it's a blur. But you never lose sight of the sign. You figure out a way to see it. I don't say anything for minutes, watching it do its tricks. I stare at Grace, slack-jawed.

"It's incredible!" I say. "You're a Da Vinci! A Tesla! Grace, it's fantastic."

"Click," Grace says after a bit, and when I do, another page unfurls and I'm not sure what to say. The very fact that she's gone ahead with all this without consulting me is simultaneously irritating and a relief. When I begin to look at the page more carefully, I feel the hairs on the back of my neck stand up straight. "Grace, it is a miracle. This is exactly what I had in my notes!"

She smiles neutrally. I click on the features, none seem operational yet, until Grace points me to the Peace Room (my precise words!). There, before my astounded eyes, is a chatroom where an actual discussion is already taking place!

sane 1: bt u cn't tlk abt peace w/ot justice.

shanti: That's taking something much more spiritual and making it political.

sane 1: ths s y we nvr gt anywhr, fckhd! if i've gt evrythng n u've gt nthng, n i sy lt's lve in peace, ds tht mke sns to u? ds it?

shanti: If you truly understood peace, it shouldn't make any difference.

sane 1: erth to shanti. erth to shanti...

The lively conversation is interrupted by an even livelier joiner.

wHiteriGht: SCREW ALL YOU PINKOS! WHITE IS MIGHT! WHITE IS RIGHT, MOTHERFUCKERS!

shanti: May you be at peace, wHiteriGht.

sane 1: yuk. ot fr nw...

"Wow!" I say. "Wowarama!" I get my notes and show her the pages where I outlined exactly the functions that she has executed. "See? Peace Room! It gives me the chills. I mean, it's downright occult."

Grace scans my notes and sets them on the table. "Not so strange, Bob. You had these notes last time we meet. Look, 'Peace Room,' my handwriting." She points to the words and they are, upon inspection, her script. "We discuss, and then I think and then I wait. And I pray. And I wait. I stop thinking. I become very very heavy. Then like a ball. Then smaller and smaller to a little bitty point." She looks up, smiling. "Then explode like supernova. That is the miracle, Bob."

"Hallelujah to that, sister!"

"For two weeks I was in trance. Make list of every peace organization, every group, every church, synagogue, mosque, temple, every peace group, Middle East, Balkan, Kashmir, Ireland, etcetera, every university, junior college, anybody on web." She takes a deep breath and sighs. "Two hundred and fifty four entries. Same time I work on logo, and website, register domain name, and sent invitation to everyone on list."

"Invitation?" That hurts a little, because at least I should have been consulted on the invitation. Her English isn't the best, after all. It's no secret.

"Look," she says and the invitation comes on the screen, the logo at the top of it, almost a freeze-frame of the morphing sign, like when you spin a coin and there's a core shape in the center. The invitation itself is worded simply... but precisely, I can't deny. "Here is a list of all the organizations we have already contacted. You all profess a commitment to peace on this planet. Please come and visit us and each other. Our Peace Room is open for you to communicate and exchange ideas. We have only started so it will be a few months before all the other links and features are active. In the meantime, peace everyone."

"Any responses?" I ask.

"Enough to start."

Grace watched for activity and, to her delight, the site began to get some hits. She made sure we popped up high on Google. The chat room looked lively at first, but quickly dwindled to around five regulars, mostly sane 1's tortured attempts to impress and perhaps meet shanti (he/she still hasn't been able to ascertain his/her location). So, there was still no revenue-generating device (i.e. product or advertising), but we were certainly set up to begin.

We kicked into gear, working twelve- to fifteen- hour days developing our catalog (the logo on T-shirts, stickers, flags, cups, baseball caps, condom wrappers). I contacted Milan's friends, Trima Printers near Sarajevo and negotiated 10 percent for a break on initial costs, since our orders might be small and erratic at first. We waited and nothing happened.

Then one week the website suddenly began to flourish when a theological seminary in Dublin got into a fierce debate with a San Francisco activist group about whether peace is possible in earthly life and without God. I have no idea why, but it sparked an interest, and pretty soon the chat room was active a good part of the day. sane 1 also gave us the idea that we should run a personals listing service for peaceful people and those who want to love them. And surprising links developed with yoga schools, Buddhist meditators, Sufis, progressive churches, synagogues, and news services. We created separate sections with regional listings (up to a point) for Peace for the Body (yoga classes, Pilates, chiropractors, aromatherapists, etc.,); Peace for the Mind (more yoga classes, meditation instruction, therapists of all stripes); and Peace for Society (political activists, churches, campaigns, world news).

Yes, it was a miracle of sorts, there was plenty to do and plenty left to be done. There was only one problem: no money. Though we had days with as many as three thousand hits, nobody, no person or organization, had yet shown any interest in our wares, and all the yoga mats and balls and bricks and all the geranium oil and orthopedic pillows were being sold by other companies using our portal free-of-charge. We'd liquidated all our reserves (my five plus another three from Grace), setting up, doing the sample orders, paying lawyers for the simplest agreements. Naturally, we were working for nothing.

Don't get me wrong. I knew it could have been much worse. I just had the feeling that someone out there would see the lovely logo designed by Grace and want to wear it, hoist it, put it on their bumper. And they would be supporting a site whose services they appreciated. We're straightforward about the fact that we hope to support ourselves through the site, so you would think one of these highly evolved people would buy ONE FUCKING BUMPER STICKER! Our stuff looks good too. Trima did an excellent job. The T-shirts are spectacular, the golden emblem gleaming like a sorcerer's amulet. You'd stand for something and be super-groovy to boot. You'd be stylin', son!

"Or you get beat up," Grace says the gloomy day when we face our finances. "It look good to us, but no one want to be seen as peaceful right now. They afraid they get beat up." It's as if the exhilaration of the last few weeks finally caught up, and when we look around, we see the reality through our delirium: an entire corner of Grace's studio stacked with samples, unpaid invoices scattered on the table, designs piled up for features we won't have the money to effect.

"Want a beer?" I ask, and Grace nods. I have the odd unpleasant feeling of losing touch, like when the line snaps as you're reeling in a big one and there's suddenly the void around you. Walking to the fridge, I can't shake the vertigo that comes with the recognition of folly. "Why?" I ask, handing her a beer.

She holds the bottle with both hands, takes a baby sip. "Why what?"

"I just realized this is lunacy."

"Only now you realize?" Her smile breaks into a small chuckle.

"So why did you do it?"

"You think you the only crazy person? You arrogant, Bob."

"Sure, you're right. My fault, my fault. But did you believe it would work?"

"Of course." Taking another baby sip, she turns to me and her face is stoic again. "Is already working."

"Come on, Grace. Even if we get those ads, you know that won't pay for anything."

"Our numbers still growing."

"Yes! But we must sell something! People must buy something!"

We are quiet for a few minutes. "I tell you," she says. "When I came to meet you I only wanted the money you owe me. But for a week before I was feeling like I was wasting my life. Who knows when it will end? Die like that," she snapped her fingers softly, "I was having these kinds of thoughts. What am I doing? Am I throwing away a precious opportunity? Do you know what I'm talking about?"

Frankly, the blasts did shake some of my confidence in Bob's equanimity. Like getting hit reminds you of being hit. Reminds you there's nowhere to hide. I was afraid unless I got busy pronto, the pain I jettisoned years ago threatened to re-surface with a vengeance. The peace of mind I'd purchased and secured by banishing my history was getting wobbly. There were tremors, flashes some days, bits of the past leaking through, potent, disturbing. Working on Peace INC. might have helped avert a psychic disaster. "Sure," I say. "I know what you mean."

"I was in a very bad condition. When you made your proposal, I saw your problem." She smiles. "You will have to get better, Bob. You were too eager. You showed vulnerability. Sorry, I was not convinced."

"Ouchy."

"But even so it was an answer to my prayer. A sign. I live by these kinds of signs. And what we've done so far already makes me feel... good. We have traffic, we're known, now we must place some product... You must go out there, Bob."

I know she's right. I'll have to hit the streets. Take the mountain to Muhammad. "I'll have to get better, huh?" I say and we both laugh a little too boisterously, trying to drown out the knowledge we are flat broke.

Money, money, money, the Frankenstein monster that corrupts men's souls. The irreducible value. The current godhead. The Golden Fucking Calf. What makes the world go round, etc. All thrillers owe a great debt to Karl Marx: you want the story, just follow the money.

I'll have to have the M-talk with Elena. I've completely ignored my domestic responsibilities (and costs) in the whirlwind of the last few months. She hasn't pressed either, which I appreciate. Clearly, she's not working, and though her rent is low (it was her mother's lease), we do have expenses. I've put some things on my card, but I know that doesn't account for our expenditures. I'm also worried because the last time we actually talked, she turned weird, started crying, and demanded, like a child, that I tell her I love her. Which I did, of course, until she went to sleep. The vibe has been fragile ever since. So, to start off on the right foot, I pick up Elena's favorite, a Cajun pizza (crawfish, peppers, andouille sausage), and gourmet cream soda.

"Honey, I'm home!" I shout, trying to muster as much levity as possible.

"Hi," comes a dear voice from the bedroom. The apartment stinks of cigarette smoke.

I set the goodies on the dining table, throw my coat on the couch, and am about to go into the bedroom, when I notice something eerie: the place is spotless. "Whoa," I say loudly. "Twilight Zone!" I push the door open and leap onto the bed next to her. "You angel." I kiss her face a few times. She pulls back, a bit startled by my pounce, then kisses me softly on the cheek.

She puts her book down and holds me in a tender gaze. "It took the whole day."

"I'll bet. I got your favorite, Cajun and cream soda."

"Sweet. Come on. I'll show you."

She takes me on a guided tour of the apartment, pointing out the details of her obsessive labor, the dusted tchochkes, spotless vegetable drawers in the fridge, gleaming grout between the tiles in the shower, stacks of freshly laundered towels and sheets. "I even did the curtains. Feels good, doesn't it?" She hooks my arm as though we're walking a promenade, leaning her head on my shoulder. She is truly adorable in a Peace INC. T-shirt and I feel aroused for the first time in weeks. "Let's eat," she says. "I'm starved."

We sit down at the table (now clear of the Babel of junk I'd piled on it), and Elena pours the cream soda into champagne glasses. When she walks past me she pecks the top of my head. It's been some time since she's been so casually affectionate. I know all this should make me happy, especially since we will have to discuss some grim realities, but I'm spooked. "How's the script?" I ask.

"Moving." She's not looking up from her plate.

"Excellent. Super. Super."

"Anything new for you?"

"No, not really. Well, it looks like we'll get some banner ads... But I don't think it'll make any difference."

"Meaning?"

"Meaning we're broke." The admission to Elena unleashes my suppressed feelings. I watch Elena allow me a moment by focusing on her food, and my despair gives way to lust. I see a corner of her bare thigh under the table; I want to devour her.

"What next?" she asks calmly.

"Oh, who cares," I say, going over, kneeling next to her, cupping her thighs, my head in her lap. She strokes my hair. "This I like."

"There's something I want to talk to you about," she says. I feel a blade flying down a guillotine.

"Oh." I sit up.

"Don't look so worried."

"Alright."

She stands and I can't prevent myself from peeking under her T-shirt, momentarily taken by her hearts-and-angels panties.

"Okay." She lights a cigarette, paces, puffing, intensely staring at the ground; she's struggling mightily to get the words just right. Then she stops in mid-stride and stares at me, or more accurately, through me, her cigarette poised next to her mouth. "Okay," she says again, this time light-hearted like she's worked it out. "Relax, Bob. It's not that bad. Don't worry, my sweetie." The last in the tone of a consoling mother, coming up to hug me, smothering my face in her breasts. I almost make a grab for her ass but think better of it.

She joins me sitting cross-legged on the floor. We like the pow-wow. It's one of our forms. "I have money."

"What?"

"I have money."

"From where?"

"Grandmother in Germany."

"That's fantastic! Elena! When did you find out?" A small pause. "How much, may I ask?"

"Enough." There's a chill in the room. I feel its sting.

"You won't tell me? You're kidding."

"No. I don't think it's appropriate."

"Must be a lot," I say, laughing. She does not laugh with me. Now I'm troubled because I feel there are ramifications I can't guess. "When did you find out?"

She keeps silent for long, dense seconds. "Ten years ago."

"What?! Ten years ago? You mean the whole time we've been together you've been... rich?"

"Not rich." It's the first time she's ever sounded like a rich person. "I have some money, that's all."

I'm livid. "So all this time you're giving me hell about my so-called past, you've been holding a rather important piece of information! It's an outrage! A travesty! That you would try to take a higher moral ground! I at least put it on the table. Take it or leave it. But this is... this is... a lie, it's a betrayal!"

"Calm down."

"I will not! All those romantic boho moments, scraping together quarters for OJ, all the odd jobs, all the complaining and commiseration, all totally false! Me playing the fool! A buffoon for your amusement! I can't believe it!"

"Are you through?" she asks. I roll my eyes in disbelief. "First of all," she continues calmly, "if you paid even the slightest attention to what things cost, you'd see even with this lease, there was no way I could afford the kinds of things I buy, even when I worked two shifts at Ponchos. You were with me when I bought those boots for five hundred. So, you knew, Bob. It was only convenient not to know."

"I..." I couldn't say anything. Of course it perplexed me. I just thought she was thrifty in ways that weren't evident. She didn't spend much on food, for example. Yes, I knew something was off.

"I'm telling you now because... well, because I see... I see how much this," she points at the Peace INC. T-shirt, "means to you. And because... you loved me not knowing I had any money. Understand?"

"What are you saying, Elena?"

"I can give you some money."

"Forget it."

"You're upset now. We'll talk about it later."

"Thank you, Elena. Thank you for offering, at least." I lean over and kiss her lips. Her response feels perfunctory. I put my hand on her smooth thigh and she takes hold of it, kissing my fingertips. No go, amigo.

"Want to see a movie?" she asks. "My treat."

Back to normal. I remember how confused everyone was by what it meant. There was a much hyped existential crisis. People with families renewed ties and got weepy about passing time. There were terror marriages and terror break-ups and terror sex. Walking up the main avenue on a brisk, sunny, winter day, all those anxieties feel like part of a dimly remembered nightmare. Terror still fills the news, of course. People may be shaky inside, but don't show it. Anthrax, bio-chem, baby-nukes, dirty bombs, suicide bombers, occupy a looser psychic orbit, visible for frightening glimmers, then blessedly gone. Maybe I'm only projecting.

So why do I feel good? A boost of cash flow and the world appears through rosy lenses? Partly true (naturally I accepted Elena's offer). I also feel good for reasons that per-tain to the quality I am marketing: because I'm not being bombed or shot or tortured or starved. The avenue is peace-ful. People stroll under the bare winter branches peacefully. A Scottie sniffs at a bench peacefully (until he pees on it, at least). It's obvious, yet I'm struck by how rare a feeling this has become. Or was it always so? Ancient fratricides, patricides, matricides, blood-feuds. Do we not evolve, or as some ancients believed, is it one long devolution? If these peaceful people, myself included, found themselves in cir-cumstances where they were being bombed or shot or tor-tured or starved, how peaceful would they remain?

There's been no real snow this winter; the holidays, supercharged already, were balmy and strange. Elena and I didn't do much special. We stayed in when we weren't working, watching TV, *It's a Wonderful Life*, for the zil-lionth time and thinking it better than ever. Apparently they had to fight the censor board, because Potter, the bad guy, is never punished in the movie. There will always be Potters, says the quintessential optimist, Capra. We also watched several versions of *A Christmas Carol*, including the moving *Mr. Magoo*, and that particular story too had extra punch, magnified by events. In the George C. Scott version, Scrooge, who is more cynical and wry than the traditional crabby portrayal, is taken by the Ghost of Christmas Present to witness the plight of a pauper family. The Ghost opens his robes to reveal two spectral, sickly children, eyes wide. "These are Ignorance and Want," the Ghost says. "Together they spell Doom." And I trembled with Scrooge and thought, bless you Charles Dickens (Elena assured me it was true to the book), you can still scare a grown man.

But I am alive, and that is the point. My faculties are working. I am loved... I think. I am on my way to meet Milan at an Indian vegetarian eatery. I want to take this moment of relief, and attend to what I've been neglecting. Well, with Milan, in this instance, it was more avoidance than neglect. It makes me sick if I think about it. When Peace INC. was just getting started, I met with Milan to tell him about my plans, and I could see the moment I set eyes on him he was in a sourpuss mood. Before Anna, before the Buddha, Milan was a terribly cynical fellow. Nihilistic, in fact. He once told me a story of playing Russian Roulette at boarding school. For real, with bullets. Once in a while, you'd notice the old personality resurging. I can't put my finger on it, a quality in the eyes. I noticed, but I'm determined not to pay it too much heed, treat it like a medieval demon, and give it no attention. So I launched into my pitch, and I think I was really cooking. Milan slouched back in his chair, chewing his coffee-stirrer, and when I'd finished, he laughed cynically (like a mean boarding-school boy, in fact!) and said, "I can't believe Grace is going along with this. Is she insane?" He did some truly gratuitous back-pedaling, mostly apologizing for what he said, not what he'd believed. I listened patiently enough.

When he was through I thanked him for his support, and as I turned to leave, I said (God help me!) "Loser," under my breath. On my honor, I did not mean for him to hear it. I was angry, blowing off steam. I called him a few days later and he was polite but cold. I didn't ask whether he'd heard me. I couldn't figure out how to do it. Since then, we've exchanged one message each on the answering machine. Technically, it's still his turn, but I called for the meeting.

I almost miss the place, the entrance is so inconspicuous. I know I'm early, but Milan greets me with a nod. I join him at the cramped table. The space is as narrow as a shoebox and the food on display in the deli containers looks fresh, tasty. The tables are packed with cabbies. "Kosher too," Milan says, smiling.

I reach over and slap his shoulder in a comradely fashion. "How've you been, my friend?"

He looks tired, beaten down, yet manages a smile. I can't help noticing the demonic gleam in his eye is undimmed since I saw him last. "Surviving." The chubby waiter comes and I defer to Milan's expertise. He orders many savory delights. As the waiter leaves, Milan clasps his hands together on the table. "I am sorry for reacting the way I did. About your idea."

"Don't sweat it. Everyone's entitled to an opinion."

"No. Listen, Bob. I'm very sorry... I talked to Grace, and she told me it was going well."

"Going well... ?"

He smiles. "At least that it was going."

"Fair enough. Actually I feel pretty good about it at the moment."

The waiter comes with a tray of what looks like rolled pasta, chilies, and mustard seeds. I pop one. It's sublime.

"So, you find some revenue?"

"Yes." I continue eating. I don't want to elaborate the details.

"What happened?" His tone and expression make it clear he's happy for me.

"Well... I... Elena bought a stake in the company. She saw how it was going, and thought it would be a good bet."

"Elena? Where did she get money?"

"Long story. Some other time. My point is it keeps us alive."

"Right," Milan says, distracted. We continue eating in silence as the waiter brings one delicacy after another. Milan coughs and his face turns crimson. He drinks some water, leaning back to recover. "Chili," he says, his eyes running tears.

"They're something."

"I don't know, Bob." He's looking at a postcard of the Swiss Alps under the glass-top table.

"What?"

"You want to know what I truly think, right?"

"Yes," I say, with some trepidation, because the gleam is at full intensity. His head is darting around on his neck, staccato, like a bird.

"As a business, what can anyone say? If business makes money, it's good business. If you figure it out, excellent. Good for you. But it doesn't sound like that is happening, from what you tell me. As an idea, though, I have to admit, I find it... you want it straight, right?"

Of course, asshole. "Sure."

"There is something deeply offensive about taking something like peace, and making it into a commodity, like potatoes or toothpaste."

"I'm not selling peace. Of course you can't sell peace! You can be reminded of peace, though, Milan. You said it yourself. What you read in the Dalai Lama. Every being wants to live in peace."

"Don't drag His Holiness into this, Bob. You're up to something completely different."

"Are you sure?"

"Yes," he says, crossing his ankles. He holds the salt shaker, staring at it like Hamlet at the skull. "You are trivializing something much deeper than your understanding of it. Do you have any idea how difficult it is to be at peace for even one second? Do you? This is what His Holiness is talking about. You only have peace when you overcome greed, ill-will, and delusion. That is very, very, difficult. Taking a spoon to the cliffs of Dover. Countless lifetimes of practice and dedication... Not just wearing your fucking T-shirt. Sorry, but I'm telling you how I see it. Even to be in touch with the suffering in the world, to actually be aware, that even this meal we eat is at the cost of violence and suffering. All the insects and worms and plants that are killed and mutilated under the plow, just for us to eat. And that's a vegetarian meal. To truly feel it is inhumanly difficult. Much less aspiring to peace. Desire is the enemy of peace, Bob. And you're motivated by desire."

"What else is a person motivated by, Milan?"

Milan looks up and I think he's going to cry. "Compassion. The tradition says compassion. The well-being of the other. Buddha and Christ."

"Milan, you are speaking of spiritual perfection. I'm talking about making a living. How could I possibly compromise peace, anyway?"

"Come on. Happens all the time. Always in times of war. We go to war for peace, right? Isn't that the upside down world? You can compromise peace. Sure you can. You know what else I think?"

"No, what?"

"I think basically you don't want to grow up. You don't want to get a real job. Deal with any real responsibilities. Hell, you don't even want to share your past with the people closest to you. You don't really care about anybody else unless they serve you in some way. Look, I'm being straight because I care about you, Bob. I think you can accomplish all kinds of things..."

Milan goes on in this vein, weaving tough love with diatribes on the human condition, recommending various meditation techniques, retreat centers, and the like. I don't take his character assassination seriously because I can see he's stressed out. I'll let him finish his lecture before happily informing him that almost everything he mentions can probably be found on some link at Peace INC.

CHAPTER IV

The fence of the old church is dense with testimonials, poems and photos, plastic flowers and multi-colored woven paper ribbons. High up someone has hung a small T-shirt sporting homemade *Simpsons* characters, a wrathful Homer grabbing a dismayed terrorist in a headlock. I'm happy to see many of the small shops are up and running, delis buzzing, entrepreneurs pedaling their photos and flags. The city seems in its rhythm again, wounded, but slowly on the mend.

I take small steps, slowing down a moment, trying to shift all my attention to my feet. Heel, toe, heel, toe, heel, toe. I can feel the energy grounding itself and me with it. I have to be calm when I go in. Energetic, but calm. My finger hesitates a moment before I ring the buzzer. It doesn't list a name. "Yes?" says a crackly voice on the intercom.

"Yes. Hello. I'm here to see Mr. Dodd. I'm from Peace INC."

A few more pops and squawks; the intercom goes dead for many tortuous minutes before the door buzzes me in. Mr. Dodd's organization, PFCW, has a long pedigree, dating back to after the Great War, the subsequent rough time through WWII (accused of siding with isolationists, then later of supporting the Axis), softer through the early Cold War (straight pinko-commie stuff), a boom through Vietnam (until more radical factions denounced them as bourgeois), and a slow decline through the late Cold War (covert actions from all sides making things complicated), and into the questionable present. They have endowments, mysterious philanthropists, that keep them going through the long periods of dormancy. I scheduled the appointment because someone from PFCW identified themselves in our chatroom, so hopefully that gives me something to work with.

I walk into the office, heartened by the look of it: a large open loft with big windows, shiny wood floors, and great light. There are a few makeshift dividers including an exquisite Chinese screen, large ancient tanklike metal desks, bookshelves lining the walls, crammed with books and files. I walk up to the nearest desk, quickly surveying the room (I count seven total, four women, three men, varying ages) and say to the cutie with the buzzcut and diamond-pierced nostril, "I'm here to see Mr. Dodd."

She looks up from her computer screen, giving me an unabashed once-over. Suddenly I'm conscious of my appearance, I feel absurdly over-dressed in my Armani suit. I was so excited about wearing it (got it for a song in an off-the-truck sale), that it never occurred to me it would be inappropriate for this particular customer base. "Sure," she says with the assurance of a gatekeeper telling me I've passed the test. "Over there." She points with her thumb vaguely over her shoulder.

"Thanks," I say and follow the general direction.

The people all look up when I pass, regarding me with varying degrees of interest and suspicion. This is clearly a place to which outsiders (especially in Armani!) rarely come. I approach a bearded man in his fifties leaning back in his chair. "Mr. Dodd?"

"Nope," he says, pointing to another partition tucked into the corner of the room.

Behind the screen sits Mr. Dodd, a clean-shaven man in his mid-fifties with an enormous bald head and tiny oval granny glasses. "Hello," I say to his piercing gaze, "I'm Bob, from Peace INC."

He is also shameless in his once over, before offering me a seat. "What can I do for you, Bob?"

"Perhaps you are familiar with our website."

"Sorry, can't say that I am."

"Well... someone from this office has spent time in our chat rooms."

"A naughty one, I hope." He makes a wry smile, releasing some tension.

"You see, Mr. Dodd..." I reach into my bag for our brochure, handing it to him. He pushes his glasses down his nose, studying it.

"Clever peace sign," he says finally. "Beautiful, in fact."

His words are, of course, the most lovely music to my ears. I am exalted. "Oh, thank you. We worked very hard developing it. You see, our feeling was that the movement needed some updating, a change in presentation, some fresh energy for these trying times."

Mr. Dodd smiles to himself, perusing the brochure. "Fresh energy never hurt," he mutters.

"So, the website is already a great success and we want to promote a whole new image for global peace, a new look, a new vision!"

"Are you familiar with the history of PFCW?"

"Yes, a bit."

"Then you know we have gone through many changes. One of the ongoing dilemmas is that our message is universal, but as we are situated nationally, we must respond to the national climate. Understand? Most recently we split again with some anti-globalization groups because our position was too wishy-washy for them. Some form of global network is unavoidable at this point, no? The question is, what kind? In service of what? Peace? Justice? Harmony? Or rapaciousness? Conflict? We at PFCW see many advantages to a global network..."

"Excellent," I say. "Then perhaps you will be interested in our approach."

"I'm not sure I understand," says Mr. Dodd. I gather from his cold stare I wasn't taken enough with his discourse.

"Yes, what you say is completely true. But you see Mr. Dodd, we are not funded in any way. We are not a not-for-profit company. The only way we can continue our work is to sell our materials... at the back of the brochure." He turns to the back pages, grinning. Somehow it isn't an encouraging grin.

"What was your name, again?"

"... Bob."

"Yes, Bob what?"

"I go by that one name."

"Like Prince or Cher or Madonna or Sting... Well, that's interesting. Any reason?"

"Long story."

"Where are you from?"

I sense the entire direction shift. I'm losing him with every question and answer. "I'm an orphan," I say to end it.

"Sorry. I was only curious about your accent."

"What accent?" I say, not able to contain the irritation in my voice.

"Well, that's why I ask. Can't place it really. Lebanese, maybe? Or Tajik?"

"By now I was hoping it would be American, to tell you the truth."

"No, that's not what I meant. You sound fine. Fine. I was only curious."

"Mr. Dodd, you said you liked our new sign..."

"It's funny," he says interrupting me. I don't know why, but I suddenly realize he grew up with wealth, and it angers me, like he's used to interrupting whomever he feels like whenever. Elena flashes in my mind's eye, in her cold, remote aspect. "I thought at first you might be some kind of secret service, checking up on us. You never know. But you would have to be extremely clever to disguise yourself as a person with one name. I mean, why would you do that?"

"I'm not secret service."

"Yes, I see. I see you aren't. And though, to be frank, I find your enterprise... dubious, I do like the new sign, and perhaps someone in the office will be interested." He punches an intercom button. "Emily, could you call the troops." He smiles. "A little pacifist humor."

"Sure," says the distinct voice of the nostril-pierced cutie. I hear footsteps shuffling, some murmuring and grumbling from behind the partition. "Let's go," Mr. Dodd says, standing. I'm taken aback by his height, at least 6' 5". I follow him to the other end of the loft, where all the PFCW staff are gathered around a circular wooden conference table. The man I'd first assumed was Mr. Dodd is still slowly making his way over. The cutie leans against the windowsill with a legal pad and a pen. It's hard for me to keep my eyes off her, and my fantasy is, surprisingly, not purely sexual, but another kind of longing, for connection, simple affection. Elena and I haven't done it for weeks, and after she wrote me the check for Peace INC., things have definitely changed. She seems happy, and that should make me happy, but her happiness seems to have nothing to do with me. As if reading my thoughts, Emily gives me a friendly smile. It is enough for me to regain my balance.

"So, folks," says Mr. Dodd. "Bob here has a company called Peace INC."

"I've been on their site," says the grumpy man with the moustache. Too bad, I was hoping it was Emily who'd visited.

"Good," says Mr. Dodd. "You can fill everyone in."

By Frank's face, I know I don't want him to translate my company to his cohorts. I also know that I shouldn't stop him. Frank clears his throat. "I don't know much about it. I went into one of their chatrooms and argued with some seminarians about whether peace is possible without God." The gathered staff all snicker.

"I'm assuming you argued it was possible, Frank," says Mr. Dodd. "I see we'll have to find more for you to do around here." More snickers, Emily merely smirks. I watch her a split-second too long, letting Mr. Dodd continue. "Well, Bob here has some... paraphernalia... you might be interested in."

Dodd, you dickhead. You could have at least given me a chance.

"Hello, everyone. Our company has many aspects, but one is that we created a new face for peace." I pause, which is a mistake. I needed more enthusiasm for that opener; it was flat. "A new look." I take a quick scan and know I'm tanking. The two oldsters literally roll their eyes, the nebbishy guy and his seeming female twin grimace like they smell something offensive, the others stare blankly, and yet, Emily still seems amused, connected. "So," I say with renewed hope, "we developed this!" I make a flourish reaching into my attaché. I hear a chuckle or two. I decide to play it nutty. "Ta dah!" I say, unfurling the T-shirt, holding it up by the shoulders. "Behold!" I flash a smirk at the nefarious Dodd, to let him I know I'm made of sterner stuff. I pivot the T-shirt slowly around the table, then lay it at the center. It works. The ones sitting get up to get a better look, the ones on the periphery move in. Even dickhead Dodd comes in close for a peek.

You see, the T-shirt is undeniably a success, the electric sky-blue, the dazzling golden emblem. Trima the printer got it to glimmer in a way I've never seen before. The damn thing is attractive! The sign is nothing to be ashamed of, either. Dodd said so himself. As they start to murmur about it, I go into the attaché again, and bring out the bumper stickers, the condoms (the insignia, plus "Make Love Not War," on them), a small flag (we do all sizes), a small poster (ditto), and the brochure listing many other items and services. "Very nice," I hear, "Beautiful," and, "Interesting." I can't keep straight who says what because I'm fixated on Emily. She's studying it closely, then backing away, squinting her eyes, tilting her head, with a seriousness that's making me over-excited. "Cool," she says, softly, and her voice itself is cooling.

"This is your business?" asks the oldster woman with a long gray braid. No doubt there is condescension in her voice. Yes, Madam. You see, I am not rich! I am not funded! That does not make me lesser than you! "It's the hope," I say.

"Yes," says Dodd, laughing for no reason. "I'll leave you to it." He turns, loping back to his nook. "How much?" asks Emily.

"Depending on the order," I say pointing at the brochure. "All quite reasonable."

Emily persists in her knowing smile as she checks it out. "I'll take three T-shirts," she says. "And ten bumper stickers."

Oh, how sublime is the most ancient feeling of taking your wares to market and making a trade! The validation! And how exhilarating too, that lovely Emily will take our little babies into the world! "Excellent!" I say, writing it down. "Anybody else?"

Five out of seven place orders for T-shirts, stickers, posters, and a sample box of condoms. Only the nebbishy twins walk away unimpressed. Thrilled out of my head, I write it all down. When I look up I notice everyone has returned to their posts. Emily is already tapping the keys on her computer. "I'll have it to you by the end of the week," I announce. "Great," says Emily, not looking over. For a few seconds I stand paralyzed, listening to the clack of keyboards, my euphoria teetering on the brink of another crash. I go back to see Dodd, popping my head around the partition. "Thanks again, Mr. Dodd," I say to keep relations copacetic. "Sure there's nothing you'd like to order?"

"No, thanks," he says with a pained smile.

"Okay." I wave goodbye.

"Um, Bob?" He lowers his glasses on his nose, peering up. His giant head looks like the moon in children's books.

"Yes?"

"I'm sure you have excellent reasons for your one name, but I would give it some thought before your next meeting. It could make some people uncomfortable."

"It didn't make you uncomfortable. In fact, Mr. Dodd, it actually helped persuade you that I wasn't a threat."

"Yes, Bob. But not everyone is as paranoid as me."

"Hello, Grace?"

"Yes?"

"Sitting down?"

"Okay."

"First sale! Nailed it! They loved it!"

"You kidding. Really, Bob?"

"Yeah baby!"

"What? How much?"

"Well... You know, not bad."

"Number, Bob."

"Christ Grace, let's at least enjoy the fact for a moment."

"I'm happy, Bob. Very happy. What's the number?"

"A hundred and eighty three dollars."

"Total sale?"

"Yup. It's not so bad."

"Are you sitting down?"

"Okay."

"We got an e-mail order." She laughs, bubbly.

"What? You're kidding. Fantastic! Who? Where? How much?"

"Well... not bad also. About six hundred bucks."

"Hot damn! How?"

"I did some things."

"What things? Grace we should discuss these matters. We're in business together, remember?"

"Why you unhappy? It worked out good."

"Because... oh forget it. So?"

"Month ago, I did some research into Europe."

"Meaning?"

"I was looking at T-shirt and I thought it's good for Europe rave."

"Rave? Like clubs?"

"Yeah. You know, it has that kinda look. So, I track down the big shops, Amsterdam, Berlin, Paris, London, Madrid, Ibiza. I send free sample package."

"Free? Grace, those kinds of decisions..."

"So, shop from Amsterdam name Equarius order T-shirts and condoms. Already make back investment."

"It... it's good, Grace. I just wish..."

"Be happy, Bob. We make our first money."

"You're right." I say, my perspective quickly readjusting to sanity. "Hurray for us!" What Grace says is absolutely true. This is nothing but good. "I'm going to get a drink! And I will toast my brilliant partner!"

She giggles on the other end. "I already a little drunk."

"Grace! I'm shocked!" And I am, sort of, since it's still daylight.

"Okay, Bob. Enjoy."

Roughly seven hundred and eighty three dollars. Subtracting materials, labor (not ours, of course), and shipping (to Amsterdam), our profit is around... two hundred and change. The realization is dismal, of course, but I don't linger. We broke the ice and that's the important thing. I pour myself a Stoli, pop in the *Bee Gees Greatest Hits* and skip to track 5. I shuffle my feet to the funky synth-beat opening, then I do the Travolta strut with paint cans, checking my shoes, my reflection, my hair. I take a sip, do a spin, four steps forward, right foot twice, hand out, front, back, turn. "Stayin' alive! Stayin' alive! Huh huh huh huh, stayin' alive! Stayin' alive!" I set the glass down and get serious about the bus-stop. Left first, then right, one-eighties, three-sixties, even a few outbreaks of tango. "Huh huh huh huh, stayin' alive! Stayin' alive!"

I stop dancing, out of breath, grab my drink, and flop on the couch. If this is happiness, it is most certainly a state of agitation. Then I come crashing back down: Where is Elena?

She has claimed, at various times in the last month, things were going well in her script, and also that they were terrible. Now, of course, it's normal for any artist to feel this way; to think themselves brilliant and then a moron. Artists seem by necessity both presumptuous and fickle. So I am aware her behavior is not out of the ordinary. Yet, she appears to work on the thing obsessively, hours at the café, hours at home. She's friendly enough, and solicitous; she's fixed many meals... But after she gave me money, no question, there was a marked shift. Once her secret was out, she seemed uninterested in the game we were playing. Puzzling, because for Elena to have been revealed as a rich girl, and definitely more complicated than I guessed, should make her more intriguing, not less. Maybe I simply feel duped, used as a pawn in some princess' slumming fantasy.

We still spoon when we sleep. We still kiss lip to lip when we see each other after an absence. We got drunk one night and had a great makeout session, until she broke down sobbing for some reason. The Bee Gees have turned mournful with "How Deep Is Your Love," so I switch off the stereo, and as I do I have the distinct sensation of being adrift in space, unmoored, nearly weightless. I float up to the ceiling. This is not good. "Elena!" I shout to break the spell. In a flash I know it is up to me to find her, because I was the one who lost her. Elena, I will set it right. We will set it right. In my excitement I fail to notice the time. She isn't due home for hours. I know this can't wait. Certain junctures in life are delicate. The smallest mishandling or negligence and you don't get the chance back. I grab my coat, and run out the door.

Is it spring? Did I blink for a moment and wake to re-birth? The evening smells like spring, a light breeze holding the promise of warmth, a faint perfume. Happy couples stroll the boulevard hand in hand, pointing at curiosities, peering into shop windows. Sparrows chirp wildly, announcing the coming night. I try to think through my approach with Elena, my apology in both senses of the word. Peace INC. demanded so much attention, I lost touch with my life, our life. And the money? Of course that's more awkward, especially considering my current negative cash flow situation. I can tell her we made our first sales. I can tell her initial responses are promising. I'm not even sure she cares about the money. Then why does it bother me so much? Pride, sure. Ego, sure. But also a feeling like I'm not meeting my end of a transaction. Is that what love reduces to? I give you this, you give me that, let's call it even?

I approach the block of the café, and again do my breath work, clear my mind, connect my feet to the ground. You only have to let her know you love her. Relax. It's simple. I check myself in a shop window. I notice I've mis-buttoned my coat and fix it. I pat my hair (like Travolta!). I'm waiting to cross the street when I see Elena's striking lime-green peacoat exit the café. I don't yell out, and instead decide to sneak up on her and surprise her with a smooch from behind. She almost turns my way and I duck into a doorway. When I look again I see she is joined by someone. A man. He says something and they both laugh. She touches his arm. I'm sure it's nothing, a café friend, why not? I should just walk over and say hello. I almost do, when it occurs to me that by our schedule, she is not due home for three more hours.

I look again, and they're still standing in the same spot, except now they've both lit cigarettes. Ah-ha! The smoker's break! Of course! Until I remember they let you smoke inside (Elena's foremost reason for picking the location). Elena's back is turned to me, but I can make out loverboy, and to my great dismay he is ruggedly handsome with a two-day beard and a sparkling smile. Stop it! This is crazy! Just go to her!

But I don't. I cross the street back, and pretend to make a phone call. They turn together, walking slowly north, animatedly chattering like teenagers. Is this what she wants? Puerile café banter? Trustafarians writing insipid movie scripts? Could I love someone so idiotic? What hurts me now, angers me, is I've never seen her laugh like that: open and easy. She's never shared that laugh with me. I follow at a good distance, stopping at the first roadside vendor to purchase a baseball cap and sunglasses for a disguise. They turn east, laughing and chatting, but I note the only physical contact is she playfully shoves him once (also never done with me). They stop at the light, and loverboy is really in the groove with his story, he has her in stitches. She's grabbing her sides because she's laughing so much. Then at the punchline, he puts his hand on his jutting hip and does the drag-queen triple zig-zag finger snap!

How dense I am! He's gay! Hallelujah! I feel a great relief, and think I should forget my stake-out and go up to them, but I still wonder where she will go. Are they going to a movie? Shopping? What is it that she does?

Now, my curiosity feels light, like mischief. I'll follow them until it gets boring. At the next corner, they face each other, and he places his hands on her hips. Maybe I'm wrong. Or right. Or... he kisses her cheek, she wraps her arms around him, hugging him tightly, intensely. Then she kisses his cheek, patting him twice on the chest. He crosses, waving to her as he goes. Well, no harm done. He could be a friend (although I've never heard anyone mentioned who would merit such a forceful hug). He seems gay, but who knows? Many hetero Casanovas polish their gay schtick. He could be bi. Why not? Or polymorphous. Or something.

I can't let it go. I stay well behind and watch her steady, reflective pace. She looks at the ground, stops and looks at the sky. Witnessing her solitude, I want to hold her all the more. Because I love her, and, pitifully, because I'm frightened of remembering she stands so well on her own. Isn't that crucial to Eros? The need to be needed? The need to need? Watching her watch the crimson clouds, I want to hug her, like a cat who only wants to sit on the newspaper you're reading. In the pit of my stomach I feel a space, and it is not in the least pleasant. Like remembering you left the stove on. Or remembering you're going to die. An intuition opening up a memory or buried knowledge. I too look at the sky, but I'm looking for something, a spec, a dot, moving fast towards me. Who is Elena? Even what I do know, I don't understand. And don't I know she left her last man in tatters? That she cheated gleefully with me when the poor stooge was taking all the emotional battering? Is that the job I inherited? The dreary husband, as opposed to the stunning polymorphous playmate?

In my mind's eye I see the distinct outline of the spec, like a tiny comma whirling through space, a cosmic boomerang. Elena checks her watch, picking up the pace. I see her turn by the marquee of the new movie theater. As I come up to the ticket booth, though, I realize she actually turned a little further down, past the kosher bakery. The boomerang now hurtling towards my head. Bang! She turned into... a Howard Johnsons?

What the hell? A HoJos here? This was once a desolate corner of whores and crackheads; just walking past the park next to it could scare even the most savvy. Now, as if by magic, there is a prim Howard Johnsons with a welcome sign. The twilight against the clean bricks is a picture of wholesomeness verging on David Lynch. Elena walked in there. Or did she? I check down the street and there is no sign of her bright coat. There was nowhere else she could have gone. I take a breath, go inside, and up the small flight of steps to reception. The place has the fresh feeling of new construction. The room is still unfurnished. I approach the desk clerk, a hipster in a black turtleneck. He sports a small, dirty-blond goatee. "Excuse me," I say.

"Yes?" I notice a copy of Strindberg plays on a chair behind him.

"Did you see a woman in a lime green peacoat come in the last ten minutes?"

"Sorry."

Well, that's infuriating. "Sorry you didn't see her or sorry you can't tell me?"

"Is there a problem?"

Insolent boy! "Yes, there most definitely is a problem!" I realize I'm still wearing my sunglasses and take them off. "There is an emergency and her cell-phone is not working. She must be contacted immediately!"

"Emergency?" He says it very drolly, like he's not buying any of it.

"Yes, her... her father is gravely ill."

"I'm sorry, sir. I can't help you."

I see how it is. I reach into my pocket and pull out a clump of bills. Unfortunately they're mostly singles. "It's at least twenty," I say, shoving the wad towards him.

He stares at it like it's poo, then looks up at me with more pity than contempt in his gaze. "You hang on to that," he says. I gather the bills and shove them back in my pocket. One falls on the ground. I crouch to pick it up, feeling my chest tighten. "It's alright," I say, my voice breaking. I get up to go and I can feel the clerk's eyes fixed on my back. "Hey," he says when I'm at the door. "She came through here."

I turn. He stops me, putting his hand up. "It's all I know, okay?"

"Sure. Thanks."

So what was it? Do they take separate routes to get here? Why? Maybe loverboy had an errand to run. Maybe he went to buy K-Y and jumbo condoms! Or was that a passionate farewell I witnessed? The chaste kisses more an indication of slaked lust than anything else. Maybe she is only going for a little rest after her exertions. So she can be refreshed when she comes home to work on her computer until the wee hours! Or loverboy is only one in a menagerie of playmates, all with their own little mysteries to keep princess from getting too bored! Damn! A hotel! A HoJos! I walk over to the former death-park and sit on a bench. Although the light is almost gone, two Hispanic kids are practicing 3-point shots. The small guy is deadly, hitting at least one in four. Hell! Hell! Hell! Elena, my sweet Elena, my love, my heart, my Pumpkin supremo, is mere yards away from me getting funky with who knows who. There is only one good thing about this kind of agony: It obliterates time. Ten seconds feels like hours and hours can burn up in the heat of an obsessive thought. I sit there as night comes. I watch the cars and people stream by. I see a star. I sit for two hours, until I see the bright green coat come out the door. She quickly turns east and joins the foot traffic. I recognize her tempo. It's like when I went to a porno house. Out the door and incognito as fast as possible. I get up to follow, but what's the point? It's ten minutes before she's due home and she is a ten-minute walk away (she's never late).

I sit back down and watch the door. In the two hours there hasn't been much traffic. Two families, backpackers, two couples, no single men of any age. I figure I might as well stay and torment myself some more, knowing that even if a single man exits in the next hours, I can't really be sure he's the one. And who knows, maybe I should be looking for a woman. (Elena's filled me in about her experimental phase, which she liked okay.) Then what do I do? Take the chance and follow any single person who comes out? I don't even care any more, yet I sit watching the entrance as the door swings open, and the distinct form of Milan exits the hotel.

CHAPTER V

People have a lot of notions about trauma. There are traumas which destroy life, twist it, crush it... but there are also those which help to create it. A lump of coal is sometimes traumatized into a diamond. But who cares whether a diamond is happy? I know a few things about it myself, having been twisted, crushed, destroyed, and re-created. You see, when the person I used to be found himself in the pit of despair, he thought and read much about trauma, hoping understanding would relieve his agony. It didn't. The only relief to be had was from a carefully staged act of psychic suicide.

When I remember back to the day, I see clearly how trauma works. Physically, emotionally, psychically, you freeze. Not fight, not flight, it's the third animal response: you freeze. Like a computer overload. The frozen part of you makes a hole in your psyche, and so on... I remember the poor boy couldn't find his breath. For days he feared he'd stop breathing. A tough patch, to be sure. I remember the very instant he understood what his uncle was trying to tell him: all dead. It was like a bomb of infinitely greater magnitude exploded in his mind, a neutron bomb leaving him standing while killing everything alive inside him.

I have a version of that feeling seeing Milan turn up the collar on his coat. He tucks his hands into his pockets and darts across the street. The psychic neutron bomb has removed all other living beings from my world. Now there is only me and Elena and Milan. I get up and follow him. It is unfathomable. Milan and Elena have never even met. I'd asked Elena a couple of times whether she was interested in getting together with Milan and Anna, and she always found some reason why it wasn't possible. Her unwillingness irritated me at first, but then I dropped it, appreciating the fact that the arrangement spared me a kind of stress. It also meant we could each keep some degree of autonomy, and I wouldn't be expected to join her with Jackie or her painful boyfriends (I lose track, but the last one went everywhere proudly on his day-glo skateboard! A grown man!). So, how the hell did they meet? How?

Milan turns up the avenue, he's heading to catch the train home. I keep a full block behind, the cap pulled low over my face. I feel eerily calm, or maybe devoid of feeling, numb, as I speed up to catch him. I have no plan at all when I shout, "Milan!" I'm near enough to see him flinch, but he doesn't turn. Can he make out my voice? "Milan!" I yell again, getting no response. He takes a sharp left. I toss the cap and run after him. When I turn the corner, I see he's much further along than his pace allows, he must've tried to make a run for it. "Milan! Hey! Milan!" I shout, now sprinting at a good clip. Hearing my footsteps, he finally turns, doing a very poor job of concealing his horror. "Hey... Bob."

"Hey, yourself. What brings you to the hood?" I say, out of breath.

Milan puckers his lips, raises his eyebrows, shrugs, and sputters like a movie French guy. "Just... uh... I met a friend for dinner... and... uh...".

"Oh, where'd you eat?" My tone is chirpy enough to unnerve him.

"At... uh..." He's terrible at this. "Um... that new place... " Pointing vaguely, squinting one eye, straining to remember. I hold him in a steady stare. I'm not sure I enjoy watching him slowly begin to writhe like a worm on a skillet.

"Walking to the train?"

"Yeah... sure," he says, relieved. He looks at me sideways, and I see the worry in his eyes. He knows I know something, but he's not sure what. King Weasel!

We walk slowly. "So, how's it going?" he asks.

"Excellent." My hands are locked behind my back, professorially. "Got our first sales."

"Really? Great, that's great."

"Nothing big, but it's a start."

"No. It's good news. Good news, Bob."

"I'm on my way home to tell Elena." (Oh, why the hell not?)

"Yes. Right. "

"You know, maybe I'll pick up a bottle of champagne. To celebrate. That'll be nice, right?"

"Yeah, sounds great." He's definitely picking up the pace.

"Hey, where's the fire, buddy?"

"What?"

"You in some kind of rush?"

"Sorry. I have to get home soon."

This I find particularly loathsome, deploying the wife and baby as subterfuge, cannon fodder. "Is everything okay?" I ask.

"Oh, fine. Fine. Just Anna is expecting me."

"I see... Hot doggy! Can't wait to tell Elena my news! Maybe then she'll be nice to me."

He cringes; I feel it. "Mm-hmm."

"You know," I elbow him, "Know what I mean? Nudge, nudge, wink, wink. Say no more, say no more."

He tries to laugh, but it comes out a croak, like a frog getting run over. "Yeah," he says.

"Because I tell you, when she's in the mood... Hoo Boy! She is one hot coochy mama! Downright insatiable! Like a porn star!" I'd never before spoken of any lover in these terms in my life. "She can do tricks, boy! Extreme kama sutra! Make your hair stand on end! And, she really loves my penis!"

"Hey!" We stop. He's close to cracking. "What the hell is wrong with you? I don't want to hear this." His eyes are lit up by his demons, but they can't meet mine squarely. "Jesus," he says, shaking his head in disgust.

"Sorry, Milan. I was just sharing some of my life with my friend."

"What does that mean?"

"I didn't know you were so sensitive."

"Bob, what the hell?" His upper lip is trembling, as are his arms. "What's all the weirdness about? You got something to say?"

Bravo, King Weasel! An honorable stand! But not so simple, amigo. "Sorry," I say gently, "It's been rough recently. I was just fooling around. You know. I'm sorry."

"Okay," he says like a parent who's settled a sibling dispute. We continue walking. "Sorry you're having a difficult time," he says, warmly (How cheap talk is!).

"Can I tell you about it? Can we just sit for a second?"

"Not now, Bob, I really have to get home. Anna and the baby..."

"Come on, Milan. Just a couple of minutes." I gesture to a wide steep stoop.

Exasperated, he nods, sitting on a step. I remain standing. "It's about Elena," I say gazing into his eyes before he averts them. "I think she's cheating on me."

"Oh." He's staring at his shoes.

"Oh? That's all you can say?"

He clears his throat. "How do you know?"

Not bad. On the ropes, but showing good instincts. Too bad sucka! "Clues."

His right foot starts tapping like he's keeping time with bee-bop, and soon the whole leg is vibrating at a frenetic pace. He cups his hands together, blowing into them, as if it's freezing out. It's not. His eyes, glazed, scan the middle distance. "What kind of clues?"

I smile. "First, there were the letters..."

I almost feel pity for him... almost. "Letters?"

"Yes. Well, e-mails in fact."

"E-mails?" He's going to crack any second.

"I know it's not right, but once she left her account open by mistake, and I looked. I noticed one address recur over the last two months with increasing frequency, so I opened the most recent one. Last week, actually..."

"Whose e-mail?" says pathetic melting Milan, shivering and sweating at once.

"Some guy named Archibald." I can't help from laughing. "Can you imagine? Archibald. Archibald!"

He's curling up on the step, his arms wrapped around his knees, pulling himself close into a ball. "What did it say?" he asks, almost inaudible.

"It was terrible! I'm nauseated simply remembering it. The most explicit naughty talk. Whole letters devoted to panties. S and M. Rubber, latex, enemas. I checked the other ones. It's been going on like that for months."

Now his head is resting on his knees. His whole body, concise as a coconut, begins to vibrate. "Aaahhhh," he erupts, standing straight, the veins in his forehead bursting green.

"I'm just kidding."

He glares at me. "You're nuts," he says, walking away swiftly.

"I know, you fool," I say to the back of his head. He stops, takes another step, stops. "I saw you come out of HoJo's. I saw her. I saw you."

He doesn't turn, his head drooping on his neck. His shoulders begin to jerk, and I can hear him cry, gasping for air, like a big baby.

Milan is dripping tears and snot and spit, right there on the street, begging for my forgiveness. Mostly I can't make out anything he's saying between sobs, beyond the fact that he's very very sorry, and he's worried he's cracking up. At one point, to my dismay, he almost collapses to his knees, grabbing at my coat sleeves. I don't react too much during the operatic outburst, saying nothing at all. What's the point? Let him exhaust himself, and then we can take the temperature. "Oh God, oh God," Milan is wailing, sitting on a step. "Milan!" I say sternly. I figure I better take the reins. "Milan! Get it together!"

The scolding seems to have some effect, his sobs quiet, and his body quakes in a steady pattern of hiccups signaling the end of a jag. He sniffs, wiping his face on his coat sleeve. Bleary-eyed, he risks making eye contact with me. I'm not giving him much, I know. By now it is not intentional cruelty, or withholding. My eyes must appear vacant to him, because I sure feel empty.

"Okay, Milan." I sit on the step next to him. "Here's what works for me." My tone is dead calm. "You realize anything I ask you compromises me, every demand I make is humiliating. It is you now who must try his damndest to make sense to me. It is you now who must convince me that you didn't intend to destroy me." He chokes down a small sob. "So, ask all my questions for me, Milan. If you were me... take a second to imagine it... if you were me... what would you want to know?"

Milan covers his face with his hands, his fingertips massaging his hairline (receding rapidly, I note). "Alright," he says, bringing his hands down, slapping his thighs. "Crazy. I can't describe it any other way. The whole thing. Crazy."

"Okay, Milan." Very flat. "You don't seem to understand how this works. When, what, how, why, who, etc. I will let you speak. You will tell me the truth. As you see it, of course. But you will have to do much better than crazy."

Naturally this pisses him off, but who cares? "Okay," he says, "Okay. I see. You're in your right, Bob. Let's see, when? It was about a week after we saw each other when you told me about your company. About a week later. I got a call from Elena." It's not easy for me to remain still, but I do. "Well, you can imagine, that was kind of surprising, because I'd never spoken with her, and though it was never stated, I got the feeling she didn't want to know us. I mean, we'd invited her to dinner a few times and well, you know. So, I was surprised she called, but I thought, maybe she was trying to be diplomatic, since my last meeting with you ended somewhat badly. After you called me a 'Loser,' I was in no rush to see you. Anyway, I thought she was trying to mediate. She asked whether I'd meet her for a coffee, and I agreed. I still had no idea what was on her mind. So, we met. And..." He looks over, hesitating.

"Truth," I say.

"Well, it was... it was... crazy..."

Again that ridiculous romantic word. "Just the facts, Milan."

"There was some charge immediately between us. What can I say? That's what it was. A current. We both felt it." I'm hurt, but I asked for it. "We sat down and after a few pleas-antries, she came to her point: you." He glances at me again awaiting a response I don't give. "She said she'd tried every-thing she knew to get you to share your life with her, and it was driving her crazy, and you didn't care." I shuffle but remain silent. "That's what she said, okay? That she tried to tell you how it was tormenting her. You couldn't hear her. She understood why you made your choices, but it was still driving her slowly crazy. So, since I'd known you longest, she wanted to know whether I knew anything more."

As sick as it is, I'm mildly comforted by the fact that I drove her to him. Mildly, for a bittersweet breath or two. "Of course I couldn't help her in any way, but we started talking about it... you... I mean, how each of us has accepted it as a condition of knowing you. For me, it's nothing burning. Otherwise I would have pestered you. To me, what you are is nothing different than anyone else. Maybe more extreme, but not essentially different. Every person chooses how much of themselves to attach to their name. A man has the right to his own past. Many of us have done things or have had things done to us we'd rather not carry around." Another pause for a reaction that doesn't arrive. "I suppose it's different if you are in love with someone." What is he saying? She's in love with me, and fucks him? "Anyway, it was much worse for Elena." I hate him when he says her name. I could kill him with a hammer.

"We talked for a few hours and parted, not even shaking hands. She told me not to mention our meeting to you. Which made sense, of course. And then..." He's staring at his shoes again! "And then I said to her, I'm not telling anyone about our meeting. I said it before thinking, and knew the moment I said it, I'd acknowledged something dangerous, crazy..." Grrrrrrrrrrr. "... but I let it go, Bob. I tried to forget about it. She called again."

I spring up. The way I feel, it's for his protection. "What the hell, Milan?! What about Anna?! Devi?!" My hands are clenched into rocks. I open my fingers and take a long breath. "What about me?" I say, disgusted I am crying. "Huh, you dickhead? What about me?" I sit back down and let him put his arm around my shoulder. "Sorry, sorry, sorry..." he keeps repeating autistically.

I'm surprised I cry as hard and long as I do. I can't shake the feeling life is only one loss after another. After many minutes the cathartic boo-hooing feels like it's getting out of control, so I exert great discipline to rein it in. We sit quietly (and it is actually peaceful for moments) until Milan resumes, "It's bad. I know it. Elena knows it. But something happened between us, Bob, like nothing before in my life. I love Anna, God knows, I love her. I know how great she is, how beautiful, smart, kind. What a good mother she is. How sexy. I love Anna, our family... and I love you too, Bob, although you may not want to hear it... None of it made any difference. Shall I tell you?"

I nod. I feel soft as a marshmallow, tender as a new shoot. "You know I'm basically cynical. Right. Anna is the opposite. Now, she's not stupid. She sees the suffering in the world, the hopelessness, cruelty, but she's not in the least cynical. Opposites attracting. But in a sense, as any way to live, her approach is superior. And I was powerfully drawn to it. You know, to me, Anna was a salvation of sorts. I felt she saw things more correctly. So, I set about trying to correct myself, not only to win her, but because I saw no point in living life with my miserable attitude."

"She got you into Buddhism."

"Bob, please... She didn't get me into anything. I'm not a teenager. I became interested in her practices and started reading some books... well, you know. Yes, that was certainly part of it. I never talk about it, but as a child I was very religious..."

I don't know why this makes me laugh. It makes Milan chuckle too. "Seriously," he says. "For a while, when I was around fourteen, I used to go to church every day."

"I gather this is before the Russian Roulette period."

"You could say the one easily led to the other. I was very religious but I had eyes, I could see, and of course, I was going through puberty. Lethal cocktail. When you grow up in Europe, history is unavoidable. The war never ended, right? The conflict mutated, splintered, re-configured, but it never left. So, I was not naïve in that sense. But when I was around fifteen, I read a story about a Serb boy who was thrown into a Croat camp with his family during the war. The story was of how he lost his family, one by one. It was told very matter-of-factly. Now, these were things I already knew about, it was not news, but it triggered something very deep. Not a thirst for revenge, or anything like it. It provoked a complete collapse of my faith. How can I believe in a God that would let this happen? Pretty classic, huh? I mean, of course everyone dies. The deaths didn't haunt me as much as the boy who went on to remember them..." Does he realize who he's talking to?

"Sure, I went on to study mechanics, philosophy..." he laughs, "in other words, I never really answered my despair. I knew more, but that only confirmed my cynicism. Until Anna... until..." A few tears. "... her lightness. And also the teachings."

"Ho! This is a new one! The Buddha made me do it!"

"Come on, Bob. Don't be a jerk. I'm trying to tell you something. I knew I had to give it my best effort. I joined Anna for talks and meditation retreats, I was very disciplined about my own practice. I really felt like I'd solved something. You remember?" I nod. "And so... maybe more than anything, meditation exposed a part of my mind—a significant part—that I was previously unaware of. It peeled off a layer of my subconscious. And... and..." His lip is trembling. "I tried to deal with it, you know, sit with it, understand it, I tried to see through it, detach from it... I mean, when that layer peeled back what confronted me, that is me, was a terrifying sight, Bob. I saw how deep my wounds are. How insane my selfishness, my cravings, hatreds and delusions. How infinite they are..."

"Milan. This is all very fine. But let's be real. You wouldn't have called but she called you, is that it?"

My concreteness is no doubt tweaking his narcissism. He takes a moment to mull it over. "Bob, I'm saying it's more complicated than that. Look, when she called the first time, all the problems I was having were raging in my brain. The only time I felt any peace was playing with Devi. Anna and I had become estranged. I became embarrassed about my mental state... guilty... messed-up. When I met Elena, it was the first time I felt free to be natural... understand? Flawed... corrupt, even."

"Bully for you!"

"You said you wanted truth."

We're silent again for minutes. "What now?" I ask.

"It has to end."

"What does?"

"Me and her, of course."

"You don't sound convinced, Milan."

The infant bursts out bawling again, saying, "Oh God, oh God, oh God..."

Not encouraging. "Milan, we'll talk later. One thing. You don't call her now and tell her about this talk." Sniffing, he looks up. "Comprende? You let me handle it." He nods, his brows knitted. I jump up, run down the steps, heading for my house. My stride is purposeful, bordering on alarming. I can feel Milan watch me. Let the boy fret a little.

Milan says he was religious as a child, and he seems an adequate illustration of how a blessing is simultaneously a curse. The boy I was had no such problems. He was religious in a moderate way like his family, celebrated the traditional holidays, felt real awe in the face of mystery, prayed fervently when frightened or overly desirous. He was a pretty normal fella. He never thought about God much; it didn't come up. But after... after... in the crisis, he naturally thought about God quite a bit, tormented in a different way than Milan, because his sanity depended on it. And God was not forthcoming with answers. It wasn't like the tacked-on ending of the Book of Job where he gets everything back, only better, and his friends are punished to boot! No, there were no answers, no plenitude of cattle and wives and children. And unlike Milan, the fella I was couldn't afford cynicism, couldn't sustain nihilism. He most definitely wanted to die. Needed to die.

And now? I'm fine with God, you know. It's a personal thing. I'm a pluralist. Whatever rocks your boat, just don't bother other people. It's hard to take the socially organized part of it very seriously. Too lousy a track record. The great Bob (Dylan of course), recently said that with all the other descriptions of God we should also accept God the arbitrary. I understand there are forces beyond my understanding. I got no problem with that. Rushing home, however, my cranium aflame, it feels the opposite of arbitrary (though the great Bob is ultimately correct). It feels like God yet again has me in his sights, in the crosshairs. And somehow my faith is supposed to be that the dissolution of my self-esteem, and my personality in general, is in the interest of the evolution of the species. You die. You're re-born. Then you die again, says God the sniper. You think you got it figured out? There's a bullseye on your scalp, son!

Elena, Elena, Elena… I turn the key to the front door. I stop in the hallway, taking a moment to collect myself. I see my anger in the back left corner of my skull, a spiky orange throbbing blob. I am, without question, the wronged party and yet I feel guilty for wanting to confront her. Is that normal? Masochistic? I take the steps slowly, trying to steady my racing heart. I open the door quietly, and hesitate. In a lurid vision I see Milan banging away at Elena as she moans in ecstasy. I'm going to vomit. My eyes water, then it passes. "Hey," I say, shutting the door.

"Where were you?" comes the voice from the bedroom. The cigarette smoke seems thicker than usual.

"Sorry. Got held up. Great news though." Who am I punishing now? I go to the bathroom, and nonsensically wash my face. No tricks, I decide, no games, no torture. In the bedroom, I find her in bed with her laptop open. "Yup. Our first sales." I say.

"Really?" She appears genuinely happy. She puts her laptop aside, springs out of bed, giving me a hug and a kiss. "That's wonderful, Bob. Those peace guys you went to see?"

"Them and others. Not big, but a start. We at least know there's some interest."

She walks back to the bed, lighting another cigarette. "I had a feeling."

"What feeling?" I sound sharper than I mean to.

"You know, that something would happen with this. Grace did a really excellent job."

Everything she says is true (or at least kind), but I can see the spiky orange blob begin to pulsate. Elena is sitting cross-legged on the bed in her favorite black silk slip, her hair sloppily piled atop her head, wearing cat-eyed glasses she sometimes wears... She looks every bit the Polish house-wife (her face is capable of epic blandness), and I find her unbearably beautiful, wanting nothing more than for her to be my Polish housewife. Am I the one that got boring? I go over to her and put my head in her lap. She smells like flow-ers. The shower at home, the cover-up. It makes me think of Milan, the HoJos, her legs flying up above his shoulders like wings. "Elena, just tell me," I say. I am so fed up I could easily drop dead.

She's stroking my face, my hair. "What, sweetie?"

"Please. Tell me what's going on. Please."

My eyes are closed, the fireworks and starbursts behind my lids mesmerizing. I would like to lose myself in the show and drift into sleep. Wake up to a nice world. Wake up to my own brightness. Leave one dream and enter another. She leans and I hear her stub out her cigarette, then take a quick sharp breath. She clears her throat. "Oh Bob," she says, "Oh honey... I'm sorry." In the enormous space of my skull the words echo, reverberate, disintegrate. I hear her take a deep breath.

"Something has happened, Bob. It's serious." She gently cups my head, easing herself out. My eyes stay closed. I'm focused on a blue point, brilliant in the pitch black. The lighter clicks, once, twice, the suck, the exhale. Her foot-steps pacing... "I've cheated on you." I'm a corpse. "Bob? Did you hear me?"

"Yes."

"I said I cheated on you."

"I heard you."

"You're... what, exactly?"

"I'm hurt, Elena. This is how I do hurt."

"I'm very sorry, Bob."

"I'm sure you are."

"It was with Milan."

I can sense she is standing directly above me, studying my placid face. "Well, that's sordid."

"Bob, what is this act?"

"This is no act, Elena."

"Come on, Bob. You're in shock?"

"Maybe."

Long pause... "Do you want to talk about it?"

"Do you love him?"

One second is too long, and she takes three. "No."

"Do you love me?"

"I think so." Not the best answer, but delivered immediately.

"So I'm still alive," I say, sitting up. Elena is tucked into the comfy chair sideways, her legs sexily draped over the armrest. I see her face is cascading tears. "That's a three-second 'no' versus an immediate 'I think so.' I'd say the smart money is on 'I think so.'" She smiles, taking her glasses off, wiping her face on her forearm.

"Bob, it all got so bad."

"It did?" Somehow that didn't come out the way I meant it.

"Didn't you feel it happening? Didn't you feel us drifting, separating?"

"Shit! Hell! What the fuck, Elena?!" I leap off the bed, making her flinch. "Why Milan?! There's ten million guys out there. Any one of them would be delighted with your favors. Why Milan? My one real friend? Didn't you think about me even once?!" I regret the question instantly.

Elena cowers, a little theatrically to my taste, holding her hand up as though I might hit her. She looks at me with alarm. I've seen versions of this look, shortly before an outburst. "Of course, you moron!" Now she's bawling. "Don't you see? How crazy you made me? Don't you see it? It's... it's because I love you!"

"Because you love me you screw my one friend?" I have to laugh now.

"I needed something, Bob. I even begged you..."

"Alright! Alright. You want the story, you want to know who he was? It means so much to you, even though I tell you it means nothing to me. I'll tell you..." Memory unspools, like old movies, and oddly the camera is not his view but a view of him. Putting on his khaki and white uniform getting ready for school, knotting his striped tie. Playing soccer with his friends. Falling asleep on his mother's shoulder on a long train journey at night. I see his dad teaching him to ride a bike and the names of the different countries and planets in the atlas. Fighting his sister for the last sweet. The noisy bazaar and the used book stalls. Onions on an open grill. Then the film freezes, the frame melting, center out, bubbly corners giving way to pristine white space. "I'll tell you," I say again.

"No," says Elena. "No, don't. I don't want you to now."

"What?"

"I understand, Bob. It doesn't matter any more. Things have changed."

I don't like the sound of any of this. "You want to keep seeing him then?"

"I don't know." Also delivered with painful immediacy. She undoes her hair, letting it fall to her shoulders, partially covering her face. "Don't know," she says with just a little too much ease.

"Did he call you?"

"Excuse me?"

"Did he call you before I got here?"

She says nothing and I know it's bad when I count one, two, three, four, five, six, seven...

CHAPTER VI

A small brown bespectacled man with a flame of white hair studies my card. It's my third meeting today. The other two didn't go very well; Luna, a club-gear store liked the T-shirts but thought our wholesale price too high; and PN, a slightly anarcho peace group, were so nice that I gave them two T-shirts for free. Hey, that's good business too, in its own way, scattering the seeds. "Mr. Jones, please sit down," says the man, pointing at the seat across the desk from him. As I sit, he says, "I am Ravi Mehta. How can I help you?"

Yes, I got the cards printed up as "Bob Jones." I took Dodd's council. Elena had the nerve to make some comment about it, that now I was like everyone else. Common. A generic American, with a generic American Christian name. She tried to convince me that now I will be identified at least as of Christian heritage. I could no longer claim no religious affiliation. Grow up! I said. I am a citizen of this country! I have my rights! Besides, it's for the good of the business. And what's in a name, anyway, dammit? She didn't really argue much, but now she sometimes playfully calls me Bob Jones. Ha ha ha. Life goes on.

"Well, Mr. Mehta, my company, Peace INC. is slightly unusual in that it is a for-profit peace company."

Mr. Mehta flashes his super-white teeth, his hand cupped to his ear, leaning his head, "You say for profit?"

"Yes, sir. We run a website with chat rooms and links. All kinds of services, organizations, churches, synagogues, gurdwaras, mosques, temples..."

"I see, I see. Now, what can I do for you?"

I reach into my attaché and hand him a brochure. Mr. Mehta is, according to PEL literature, a fourth cousin of Mahatma Gandhi and has been committed to pacifism since his college days. In fact, hanging on the wall behind him is a poster from the movie *Gandhi*, with a rather robust Ben Kingsley made up as the famously scrawny Great One. Mr. Mehta scrutinizes the brochure, chewing his pinkie nail. He doesn't seem pleased. "Mr. Jones," he says, looking up. The irritation quickly vanishes from his face. "We are an absurd species, do you not agree?"

"Who could argue?"

"The larger the group, the bigger the problem. As a species at the moment we are not scoring high marks." I nod. "But the more we shrink it, the more we can see clearly." I have no idea what he is talking about. I nod. He elaborates, "If only you and I are trapped in a room, and there is only one piece of bread, we may try to kill each other immediately or we may share the bread and share our fate." His eyes are owl-like, magnified behind his lenses.

"In your story, there is no more bread forthcoming, I take it."

"One piece," he says, holding up a finger.

"So our shared fate would be death anyway."

"And so it is!" says Mr. Mehta gleefully. "The vast majority of humans want to get along. The ones in power create all the problems. Now most people would rather share than kill."

I'm not sure about that, but I'm happy he believes it. "Alright," I say.

"You're not convinced."

"I'm not sure it's realistic."

"You hit it on the head, Mr. Jones. It all depends on what you construe as real. Real for whom? Real for what? You know the story of the Dalai Lama's doctor?"

Again the Dalai Lama! How perverse the Embodiment of Compassion on Earth only reminds me of Milan and his idiocy. My chest tightens. "No," I say.

"He was a monk, of course, captured by the Chinese and imprisoned for some twenty years. Brutal conditions. He had to live on vermin and eat his own filth. So, in this time, in these conditions, he spent all his waking hours trying to teach the soldiers the Dharma, the truth of compassion. The men who are torturing him, understand. Rather than seeing his own pain, he sees their suffering. He tries to help them! Is this realistic? Certainly not by our current standards. And yet he is every bit a real human being. He was born, like you or me. But he has evolved, you see? He is the future, Mr. Jones. He is the real human. We are still only beasts."

"Yes, sir. I'm sure you're right... Did you see anything in our brochure that interests you?"

"Mr. Jones, you can see by our modest surroundings we have very limited funds." It's true: there's a door that leads to a tiny bedroom and the office/living room is cramped with two computers and cartons of files. "I have some graduate student interns, but other than that, it's only me. So... " He shrugs.

"Well... please do visit our website at least. It's free." I smile, reach into my attaché and hand him a few bumper stickers.

"Thank you kindly," says Mr. Mehta, squinting at the stickers. "The sign is quite beautiful," he says. I get up to leave. "Mr. Jones, I must admit I have once been on your website. And, frankly, I found it rather disturbing. There was a big advertisement for a massage parlor..."

"Not a massage parlor. A massage institute. A combination of lomi-lomi and Swedish shiatsu. With special wat-zu. Peace for the body. What's wrong with that?" I realize I've raised my voice and it has nothing to do with the benign Mr. Mehta. It's Milan's face I see.

"I'm sorry if I offended you, Mr. Jones. But I would like to be forthright. Whatever it was, all the therapies and yogas and meditation centers, it's all good enough, but what has it to do with peace? You simply make another empty promise, that you can buy peace, like you can buy happiness, love."

"But isn't it also possible Mr. Mehta, people will value peace only if they pay for it? Like in therapy."

"I'm not certain you must pay, but as in therapy, you must certainly do the work. The more I work for the seemingly hopeless cause of peace, the more peaceful I seem to become. You know one of my interns is a sweet girl by the name of Carrie. Now, Carrie is a committed yogini, she even teaches yoga, and this poor girl is so completely consumed by the workings of her body, that she has created a hell for herself. Always talking about her spleen or her kidneys or colon, drinking juices and potions and swallowing dozens of vitamin tablets. She's as healthy as a horse, but not at all at peace. You follow, Mr. Jones?"

"I'm not sure."

"Intent means everything, Mr. Jones. Purity of intent. Something I've learned from a long, difficult life."

"Thanks," I say, offering my hand to shake. He sits up a bit and clamps my hand tightly with both of his (vigorous old fella!). His owl eyes gaze into mine. "Pleasure," he says.

"Why not a picture of the real Gandhi?" I ask, exiting.

Mr. Mehta turns to look at the poster, then back, grinning brilliantly. "I consulted on the film. It was a gift from my friend, Richard Attenborough... Lord Richard Attenborough."

I've always wondered when people decide to become themselves. For me it was a discrete moment when Bob was born, a virtual resurrection, but my case is unusual, I know. In the normal course of life, when does a person decide: This is my story? And does that story then become more and more dense, until we suffocate within it? I went to see a lecture once by a famous English professor, and as he walked to the podium I was struck by how every bit of him was so English Professor! The slouch, shuffling step, full beard, tortoise-shell frames, brown corduroy jacket with the elbow patches. Is it that at some point in his childhood he determined what an English professor looks like, and went about actualizing it? Or did it happen gradually, first the jacket, then the beard, etc., even without his notice? Intentionally or unintentionally? Does it matter?

It matters a great deal when you are betrayed. Obviously you cannot have betrayal without first having expectation, or presumption. What did I presume? That I knew my so-called lover, that I knew, in some basic way, the character of my so-called friend. It matters that I went around in the world assuming this knowledge was not variable in an important emotional sense. Not that they weren't entitled to flux and change like the rest of creation, but that there were certain traits of character I could take for granted. As the great Bob once said, "If you live outside the law, you must be honest." Well, at least when trapped, Elena was honest. Milan called her as soon as I left him on the stoop, of course. She knew I knew, etc. From Milan, that was a clear enough message of where his loyalties lay. I haven't spoken to him since. With Elena, it's more complex.

First, there is the weirdness of sex. The very night of the revelations, in a twisted effort to comfort me, Elena went sexually berserk. I was afraid at first, then reciprocated with intensity, and after the super-charged romp, which included no small amount of biting, clawing, screaming, spanking, and alas, tears, she stunned me by asking me to sleep on the couch, and on the couch I remain. Not able to rest, I whimpered some more before accepting our wild frolic as a farewell roll, and knew whatever was coming would at the very least be inconvenient. But the last week has been bizarre even by my standards. Elena continues to insist she still loves me (once she even ventured the bogus TV distinction that she loved me but wasn't sure she was still in love with me), and I was welcome to stay on the couch for as long as I liked. In a perfect world—or even an imperfect one where I had some money—I would have promptly packed my bags to shore up what was left of my dignity. Or if the situation wasn't what it is, I might have crashed with Milan until I figured something out, until Peace INC., started to generate real revenue. If, if, if...

Life at home—and what an ugly four-letter word that can be—becomes curiouser and curiouser. Elena and I have agreed that neither party will question the other's whereabouts, which I suppose is for the better. My worst hours are when I allow my mind to imagine her day. I naturally yearn to know, but I'm also aware I would be quenching my thirst with sea water. I keep a tight lid on it, which sometimes explodes in unpleasant ways, taking the form of murderous fantasies, usually involving only Milan, although the most vividly imagined one had me kicking the door down at the HoJos, blasting the both of them in the act, then putting a bullet into my own temple. So, it is a fine calibration of mind, and one I might even manage, if I were assured that there is no hope whatsoever for Elena and me. Ah, then there is sex...

Two nights ago, I came to my so-called home after a long day of hassles, poured myself a stiff Stoli and was flipping channels to forget my woes, when Elena came home looking a little blue. It is still not easy for me to ignore her emotional state, having attuned myself to her fluctuations over time. Clearly, I've missed a few crucial junctures because of my business preoccupations, but even when I was being cuckolded, I could always tell when she was unhappy, even if I was clueless of the cause. "Hey," I said, neutrally.

"Hi," she said, weary, walking into the kitchen with grocery bags. "You hungry?"

"Sure." And it would have been so natural for me to join her, tell her about my frustrating day (invoice, payment, delivery problems with Trima the printer), share a bit of my hope (small orders from Albanian and Pakistani peace groups located in Berlin), kiss her neck, chop some veggies, and so on... Instead, I knocked my drink down and poured myself another healthy dose. After a while the distinct smell of peppers roasting on an open flame started to waft through the apartment, a special treat reminding Elena of her home country. It started me again speculating about her emotional state, because she'd only made them once before, and she confessed it was because she was feeling exceedingly lonely in America. Finally, my own jumpiness was more than I could stand, so I went into the kitchen. "Need any help?"

Without turning from the stove (getting the peppers to char just right was a delicate affair), she said, "Sure. Put some water on for pierogi." I did and ventured a question, "Everything alright?"

"Ow!" she shouted, not as a response to me, but because she burned herself. The lovely peppers, yellow, red, and green were all on a plate, their skins patchy black. She was sucking on her finger. "What do you think, Bob?"

"I don't know. Seems like you're upset."

"Do you really want to talk about this?"

"I asked."

"Let's go into the living room. Water has to boil." I followed her and we sat on either end of the couch. I muted the TV. She wouldn't look at me when she said, "Milan told Anna."

I received this news with the deepest ambivalence. One part of me took some sick pleasure that the illicit lovers were having to face the real consequences of their actions. The wife and the baby carried far graver indictments than the boyfriend. The violation of contract was literal. They were real casualties. Then two other realities unfurled simultaneously: the affair was serious enough to merit his confession (I'd considered telling Anna myself, but wisely thought better of it), and beautiful Anna must be at least as broken-hearted as I was. "How did she take it?" I asked in a cool, analytical tone.

Elena looked up at me, clearly angry. "How do you think?"

"I don't know, Elena. I'd guess that she's pretty upset."

"Yeah," she said with a dismissive chuckle, "She's pretty upset. The whole situation is a mess. Horrible, horrible, mess."

"What do they plan on doing?"

"God only knows." She was picking lint off the couch. Her eyes were glassy.

"So, I gather you two plan to continue."

"Hell, hell, hell," she said punching the cushion. At that very moment, I was distracted by the TV, where the Terror Channel ran the headline that we had been targeted for a nuclear attack.

"Sorry," I said, and hit the sound button. As we listened to the news that intelligence reports had ascertained that terrorists may have gotten their hands on a ten-megaton Russian bomb and had planned on exploding it here, causing an estimated 100,000 immediate deaths and at least twice as many slow, painful radioactive deaths, Elena, now trembling like a leaf, moved closer to me, and I to her. The report dissected all the angles of whether it was right to withhold this information from the population and the local authorities, how credible the threat really was, etc. I put my arm around her shoulder, trying to calm her, although as I thought about it, I realized I was pretty unnerved myself. Her trembling turned into quaking. I had trouble holding her still. "I can't live here," she said.

I was comforting her and trying to calm myself, and my first thought was, Fine for you, rich-bitch homewrecker! Why not pick up, re-locate, and ruin some other lives! I tried to stop myself from indulging this, but my mind was running down a steep hill, with the fierce momentum of rage. "It's alright, Elena. They're on top of it," I said attempting to exert some moral influence on my pettiness. Because, at that very moment, I hated her, hated Milan, hated myself, hated the stupid world and all the stupid people in it, hated life enough to wish that somebody would just blow the whole damn planet up and get it over with.

She sprang from the couch and ran into the kitchen. I waited until the news switched to some other story, then followed her. She was emptying a bag of pierogi into the boiling water, and as I watched her stirring them in, watched her smooth pale muscular arms and shoulders flex with the motion, as I contemplated the distinct possibility that we might all go up in an instant nuclear holocaust, I felt a kind of sexual arousal I'd never experienced before. It was the yearning to affirm my animal life, to celebrate blood, bone, sinew, and it was also the chimp need to assert power, feeling powerless to control my fate. I wanted, like those sexy samizdat guys, to signal to myself that the big crazy chimps running the show couldn't subjugate me completely.

I went up behind her and turned off the stove. "Hey," she said, surprised and annoyed. I did not give her the chance to protest further. I grabbed her by the hair, hiked up her skirt, and bango! Down and dirty! We didn't speak much afterwards, eating our delicious Polish dinner (although the pierogis were soggy) in eerie silence. She later kissed me goodnight on the forehead. Our paths haven't crossed since, although I've heard her come home late and quietly go into the bedroom. The door is shut when I leave in the mornings. Crazy, to use Milan's favorite word.

I try to gauge the faces on the train, to see what effect the recent news has had on people. I can't make out anything much different: a young black mother trying to keep her two rambunctious boys in their seats; a delicate, pale, arty girl absorbed in her fashion magazine, mesmerized by futuristic sneakers; a group of ruddy Russian workers, their hands dotted with paint, their faces, even the young one, lined, eyes reflecting tragic history. Business as usual. The train comes out into the light and elevated tracks, then stops; I get out, heading quickly down the steps to Grace's. Baby-nuke or no, the show must go on!

Did I step into dreamspace? "Anna?" There she is sitting in my usual chair. She smiles, though her eyes are full of grief. "Hi, Bob," she says, "Sorry I came here. I didn't know what else to do." She sips a mug of tea. "Grace has been very nice."

"Hello Anna. I…" I smile and nod my thanks to Grace. Her mouth is locked in a bold frown, her eyes cold. "Sorry," I say to her. Then, "Hi," to Anna.

"I thought I was going nuts," Anna says. She pauses, catching herself. "Well, that's a little dramatic. I was… I was… very upset, I suppose. I needed to talk."

I turn again to Grace. "Sorry about all this."

"I'm not upset about this," Grace says.

I feel like I have no alternative but to follow up. But Anna is here. In my chair. "What's up, Grace?"

"Satan," she says, turning on her heel and marching to her bedroom. "It's nothing to do with you," she says softly to Anna before she slams the door.

"One sec," I say to Anna. I knock perfunctorily, before going in. Grace is sitting on the corner of the bed, slumped over, her face in her palms. "What's going on, Grace?"

"Satan," she says again, into her hands.

"Explain, please."

She sits up abruptly, a chunk of her black hair shooting out at a sharp angle, her eyes bloodshot. "You go deal with that," she says, pointing to the office. "Whatever that is."

For everyone's sake, I do not discuss my personal life with business colleagues. Grace has been out of the loop. "It's all terrible," I say.

"Well," she says, improbably breaking into a manic chuckle. "We talk later. It's okay, Bob." More laughing of the disturbed. "We talk after."

"Okay," I say, happy for the consideration. I go out to the office, shutting the door behind me. Anna smiles as I approach, a smile of forbearance, absurdity, vulnerability. I can't look into her eyes. "So," I say with a mechanical snicker. "We have us a situation here, Ma'am."

I am glad Anna laughs a little. "We certainly do have one," she says, staring blankly into her tea.

I sit in Grace's chair, my hands folded in my lap like I'm a shrink. I feel a bit remote too, not able to take in her pain along with my own. "How are you?"

"I'm alright, basically." She looks up again, smiling, a ray of light. "But I find I'm not handling this so well."

"There's no good way, Anna... Take a little walk?"

"It's pretty out," she says, getting up. She puts on a 50s rounded-collar brown cloth coat over her Mexican blouse and jeans. She's pretty and sad. I'm quite unsettled myself as we navigate the hallway, the stairs, the courtyard, in silence. On the sunny pavement, Anna says, "You knew?"

"I found out... I thought it was better if I didn't inform you... You know, that it might blow over, possibly... I'm sorry."

"No, Bob. I think it was right. You shouldn't have told me."

We start slowly down the small hill, the late afternoon light lending some movie glamour to the weary returning home. The spring air holds the promise of longer days and heat, roadside trees bursting white blossoms. Greeks in tight pants and leather jackets hang outside the diner, smoking, shouting, laughing, slapping each other on the back.

"What did he say?" I ask.

She's silent for many steps and then, as though she's realized something secret, she laughs. "He says he's confused. Not so original."

"And how do you take that?"

She looks to the sky. "God knows, really... I'm hurt... I'm very, very angry. Mostly that he's such a mess. I mean, he's falling apart..."

"Did he say he loves Elena?" A slim etheric blade pierces my chest, finding the membrane of my heart.

She laughs again in the gallows way. "He's not sure. Can you believe it? What a jackass. He's not sure. We have a daughter together." Her voice drops to a whisper "... a life..." The silence she leaves is thick, resistant.

"It's the same with Elena. At least the two are consistent in their mutual perplexity. But, Anna, this is all horseshit! Unadulterated horseshit! What the hell are we supposed to do? What does he want from you?"

"Time." Her stare tells me that she might indulge him, even though it is humiliating. "He knows what's at stake."

"Do you have a limit in mind? I mean, how much time, for Chrissakes?" The blood rushes to my head. I see myself throttling Milan until his eyeballs explode. Then stamping his protruding tongue with my bootheel. Surprisingly, I feel no antipathy for Elena.

"Bob," she stops, grabbing my arm. I turn to face her squinted eyes, a slash of light making her cheeks glow. "I agree. But it is also more complicated than that."

"Sure." A man bumps into me, walking past. I grab her elbow and we move onto a bench outside a narrow bakery. "It's complicated." I have a mental flash of Elena's mouth, wet and open, her glistening tongue. Then Milan's hairy back. My hands uncontrollably clench into the throttle position. "So, you will give him... time. In the interest of your marriage... Devi."

She nods. "In the interest of peace, Bob. Something you are an expert on, no?"

"Ha ha, very funny." But she's right: peace with Milan is unimaginable. Simple forgiveness feels like an insult to memory, a compounded betrayal. She shares a child with him and I don't, but I can't walk away, and forget. I realize I will have to take some action to ultimately make any dialogue imaginable.

"You know, when he's not falling apart, he's been quite nice... Nicer than in a long while."

I mumble.

"Sorry, I didn't hear you."

"If you must know, I said horseshit. But... I don't stand by it... I'm a hurt animal. I'm snarling. You know?"

She nods again. "How's Elena?"

"I should probably move out."

We're quiet for a long minute or two. "He's not a bad man, Bob. You know that too. I have to give him a chance. Otherwise, what does it mean that I love him?"

To know that Anna loves Milan still is a new kind of pain, duller, lower in the ribcage. "He sure fucked up with me. I'm not sure I can forgive it."

"I'm not saying any of it is easy. But, I've been wondering a lot what love really is. If I truly loved Milan, and I thought I did, what did I love? He says his happiness is at stake. Now, if it truly is, if I at least trust him to know that much, then he's got to do what he's got to do. Because if I love him, I want him to be happy. I at least want Devi to have a happy father, even if he's not a live-in father. See? What would I be holding onto if he's changed?"

"You may be right but I still think he's an asshole." I laugh and she joins me.

"Feels nice to laugh a little."

"Yup. A giant asshole." I laugh again, louder, but alone.

Anna's still smiling, her big almond eyes sparking mischief. "You know none of this would have happened if only you had confided your past to Elena." Now she laughs alone, and even elbows me gently to indicate that she's only joking. "Hey."

"It's okay," I say, knowing my smile is forced. "I better get back, anyway. See what's up with Satan."

"I didn't upset you, did I? I was just trying to lighten..."

"No, Anna, you didn't upset me." Which is true. The roiling in my stomach is from the inference that Milan in his mewling confessions has discussed my life with her. He definitely needs a talking to. I kiss Anna's cheek. "You take care," I say, getting up. I reach in my jacket vest pocket and hand her a business card. "My cell number is on there. Any time."

Anna takes the card, opens her worn Tibetan bag and drops it in. She finds a pen and a pad of orange post-its. She scrawls something and hands it to me. "That's mine," she says and laughs. "I just got one." She digs around in the bag and holds up a little purple Nokia, wiggling it like a puppet.

Grace is in my chair, staring into a non-space. She points to the monitor where there seems to be an article from a magazine. It's the online version of a print weekly in Amsterdam that covers the clubs: *Superfly*. I am astonished by the headline: "KIDS TRIP OUT INTO PEACEHOLES." And below is a photo of a ghostly boy raver, almost a blur except for his grin, and his ELECTRIC BLUE T-SHIRT WITH OUR SIGN CLEAR AS DAY! Hallelujah! I'm almost too excited to read the article. "Holy shit!" I say and turn to the dark and gloomy Grace. "Read it," she says.

It started in Elin and moved to Liquid. Kids falling into peaceholes. The right bpm, the right mix of chemicals, the right strobe. And the Peace Sign, the shirts out of Equarius, which, given an exact combination of these elements, glimmers in some special way, taking the traveler down a "peacehole" to the "land of peace." The ones who've taken the trip claim it changed their entire view of life. It gave them hope. Imagine that! Plus, it takes two, one to "bear the trip" and the other to "take the trip." The two make a commitment to each other. Fortunately the trip doesn't last more than a few minutes in "real time." But travelers say "peacehole time" is more elastic.

The freaky occurrence has created a run on the shirts, but Equarius, the sole distributor, assures us orders are on their way. Well, Charlotte and I say, if you can have it, even for a few minutes, go for it, you love babies!

"But Grace, that's fantastic! We're saved! Rescued from ruin!" I turn to face her scowl. "What's the problem? Didn't Equarius order?"

She nods.

"Great. How much? Big? Oh my oh my. I should call Trima. You know we should really push those condoms. There's something there that we haven't tapped. You know, a different kind of peacehole. Why not?" I'm hyper, chuckling, but Grace remains rock steady in her grim demeanor. "What's up, Grace?"

"Satan."

"What? Why?"

"You know, Bob."

"No. No, I don't. Grace, this might save the company."

"That's Satan talk."

"Come on..."

"You know it is." She has yet to look away from the non-place.

"Why? The drugs?"

Silence.

"The drugs, is that what you're calling Satan?"

She shrugs, glum.

"Come on, Grace. It's adolescence. Kids do all kinds of things. You know, rebellion, identity crisis? It doesn't mean anything. It's not like we're making them take drugs! If, when intoxicated, they interface with your beautiful design, and if this leads to what appears to be a completely happy experience, I say, so be it! It's not Satan, Grace. Didn't you ever rebel, smoke a joint at a party or anything? Even not inhale?"

"No, Bob! I did not!"

"But you drink..."

"Don't give me that. Even Jesus drink some wine. Besides, intoxication is not what I am talking about."

"Then?"

"Satan, Bob. Do you know why I did all this? Why I work so hard? Put in my money? Because I want to spread the message of Our Lord. That's why, Bob. I wanted to, in my own way, spread gospel of forgiveness and peace…"

"Yes, and to do that…" I realize I haven't fully processed Grace's religious confession, though it is not a complete surprise.

"I know, we need money. And this looks like a miracle." She stares at me squarely. "You must look closer, Bob. Because foremost, Satan is a master of disguise. You must see through it. I don't think it's good that our peace sign mixed up in drugs."

"Grace, you called Equarius in the first place! What did you expect, for Chrissakes? The *E* is for extra *E*! Get it? What did you think Europe rave was? It's fine, it's fine, it'll be a little nightlife moment and it'll pass, but our sign will have been shot into the world! And don't worry, these drug crazes don't last long."

"Body is temple of the Lord."

"Yes, but Grace, we are not condoning drug use! We could even post on our site in big bold red letters: WE DO NOT CONDONE DRUG USE! We caught a small wave, Grace. We must surf it in!"

"This all Satan talk, Bob. Go with the flow. Everybody saying it now. What flow? What if flowing in the wrong direction? Then you go with that? What if it flowing into the sewer, you go with that? Seriously, Bob, you don't see it, because you don't believe in anything."

"Hey!" I stand up. "I believe in all kinds of things!"

"That's what you say, right? That's what Milan tells me. You say you have strong beliefs."

"Milan? He talked to you?"

"Why not? I'm his friend."

"What exactly did he tell you?"

"He told me about whole mess. He was losing control on the phone."

"And how did he describe the whole mess?" The top of my head is heating up. There's a low hum in my ears.

"Not important."

"It is to me."

"No, Bob. What's important is that you build house on sand. Like Milan. Like Elena. You all groping around in darkness. Now, Satan comes to steal your own soul and you don't see it either. You say it's good for the company. You have no... no... compass. I see that, but I don't interfere in your personal life. But Peace INC. is half mine, so I have a say." She folds her arms and legs simultaneously, aggressively resolved.

"First of all," I say, pointing at her. "I think it's appalling Milan spoke to you about my life. He has no right. Secondly, need I remind you that I am the wronged party here, and whatever duress Milan is feeling is of his own making. And thirdly, what the hell do you mean I have no compass? Why, because I don't share your beliefs? Because I have given up my past affiliations? Because I would like to be simply reasonable?"

"I mean... well... you don't believe in Christ our Savior."

"See! This is what I mean! How do you know what I believe? How do you know Christ doesn't blossom in my heart? Why, because I don't tell you so? I don't make a big show of it? Or must I belong to your church, which disagrees with all the other fucking churches? Literalism is killing us, Grace! Fundamentalism is the refuge of morons! God is God is God by whatever name! Common sense! The Founding Fucking Fathers knew that! The rest is untenable and plain loco! And who are you to judge me or those kids having their own experience of bliss, even if it's delusional. If Satan is delusion itself, then your judgments are equally deluded, Grace. You can't go around condemning people to hell, even by implication. Isn't that Satan at work too? Judge not, lest ye be, etc.?"

She can't deny my logic, and she mulls it over, eyes blinking in a steady slow rhythm. "Even so, I say we shut down."

"What?! Grace, no! You're not serious... Grace, with these orders we'll actually be out of the red. A few quickly placed blurbs in high profile mags, get some buzz..."

"Shut down, Bob."

"Sure, sure. You all have your lofty fucking beliefs. Milan, with his Buddhist bullshit nonattachment. Yeah, he detached himself from his family, and attached his gonads to my sweetie! And you... you want to spread the gospel of forgiveness and peace and love, but the fact that you'll destroy my one chance to redeem this awful, awful juncture in my life, means nothing to you. Where's the love, Grace? Screw Bob! He has no protection! Being rational counts for nothing! No mumbo jumbo, no cultural baggage, no tribe, no fucking respect! That's the rule of the land now! Well, I'm sick of it! Sick and tired, dammit!" My voice breaks, squeaks, and I'm inspired to fall to my knees.

"Please Grace," I beg shamelessly, my hands clasped in prayer, "We're so close. So very very close. Please let's not shut down." Her gaze remains unmoved. I pound the carpeted floor with my fists, moaning, "Please. Please. Please. Please. Please..."

CHAPTER VII

As soon as it gets dark I make my way uptown. It's my second stakeout night in a row. I stand across the street dressed in homeboy baggies, big sneakers, and a red bandana, shuffling around to a Cachao CD (method, baby, method!). I can see the entrance clearly, but I easily fade into the background. I'm waiting for Milan.

The night's cooled off suddenly, so my streetwise samba shuffle picks up intensity to keep me warm. His entryway, next to a bullet-proof liquor store, stays busy so I pay close attention to the door. Last night I waited until ten to no avail. I'm preparing myself mentally for another long one, when, to my delight I see the weasel exit his lair. I know the silhouette, the shoulders up, head down, hands in coat pockets. It was a figure that used to gladden my heart when I spotted it at a distance. Now the charge pulls the opposite way, my heart twisting, wrung out, compressing to dust. I run up behind him, before he reaches the subway. "Yo, Papi!" I shout. Then, "Milan!"

Milan spins around, perplexed as he faces my bad-ass Latino self. "What's happening, man?"

"Bob? Why are you dressed like that?" He laughs, agitated. "You look ridiculous."

"Yo, don't be dissing me, Papi." I smile. "You got a minute? To talk."

He hesitates, staring at the ground, weighing a decision. "Alright."

"Let's step over here," I say, crossing the street, to a receded entryway. I sense Milan, flustered, following behind. With each step we take, my friend further mutates into a menace, a force set on destroying my life, a life I've cultivated with so much care, forethought, integrity. To himself he may be confused; to me he is a disease that must be flushed, a bomb that needs defusing, a terrorist who must be stopped. As Milan approaches I see an aura around him, starting to burn bright white. I lunge, my hands out where his neck should be, and grab his face instead, his nose. "Ow! Hey!" he says. I readjust to throttle his throat, and bam! He nails me in the gut. I bend over in pain, taken by starbursts. I cough. I spit.

"What the fuck, Bob. Are you completely crazy?" I look up. He's caressing his throat. I spring at him, leading with my fist, and bam! Right in the nose! His head reels, springs back. Nose bloody, eyes watery. "Arrrrrggh!" he shouts, throwing punches, coming at me. Bam! He nails me in the side of the head. Bam! Again on the jaw. I fall down. Black for a second. I see his Air Jordans. "Asshole," he says. I sit up. Milan is staggering, his fists raised still, blood leaking out of his nose. I wiggle my jaw a couple of times to make sure it's not dislocated. "Shit, Milan."

"This is seriously fucked-up behavior." His handkerchief is out, stained red but not soaked. "Savagery. Caveman bullshit."

I stand up. He jumps back, ready for another round, and I raise my hands in surrender. "Please don't tell me that your actions could be deemed civilized, by any standards," I say. "I mean, isn't that the point? The call of the jungle, and all that?"

He dabs his nose twice, checking the kerchief. The bleeding's stopped. "Please, Bob. This is difficult without gratuitous assholishness."

"Alright. Then let's be methodical. Say what you want. Then I say what I want. And we see what happens."

"Why do you sound like Robo-Cop?"

"What? You said let's deal with the situation. I am merely suggesting an easy method."

"Stop that. That, whatever that is. Coolness crap. Look, no denying we have serious situation here... I know it."

"Bully for Milan! Let's give Milan the grand prize! And what the hell are you doing talking to Grace about my life? That's messing with my business, man! That is one big no-no!"

"Come on, Bob. It was after everyone knew everything. I didn't know what to do. I needed to talk to someone. I was very torn up..."

"Poor child."

"Asshole. I was, and I wanted to call you or say something, but I... I..." His voice trails off into sniffles.

"Forget that. The question is now. The moment. Do you have anything to say... now?"

"Please drop the executioner's tone."

"Do you have anything to say?"

Milan shakes his head in disgust.

"Alright, you had your chance. So, I will say what I have to say. That is, Milan, your current state of ambivalence is no longer acceptable. I strongly encourage you to desist seeing Elena, and return to your lovely wife and daughter. Whatever has already happened has happened. I am willing to forget about it. But for everyone's sake, for your sake, for your child's sake, you must end it. It pains me to admit that you and Elena share a great passion, but remember, great passion is not love. I know that now. When I saw that I would lose her, I realized what love is. It is attachment beyond passion. All along I was not fighting for our relationship, I wasn't holding it down. I wasn't even sure how I felt once the early months of hot sex cooled off. I know some things too, Milan. I know I lost her through my own carelessness, my laziness. So, now. The moment, as it were. I am telling you to end it, and when you do, call me and tell me, and we'll go get a drink. Six months hence, you'll thank me."

A drop of blood trickles out of his nostril. He wipes it away with his finger. He actually chuckles. "Bob, forgive me, but you are a real pompous ass. You think... you think... simply because you resolve something in your own stupid mind, the world then must adjust itself to you. You don't see. You don't see whatever you don't want to see. Did you ever think of what Elena might want? Did that occur to you?"

Punching him again certainly wouldn't help matters.

"No," he continues. "Even now, when you're supposedly fighting for the relationship. Do you think of her? No. You never did. You don't see, you don't hear. And as for your fucking business. You wouldn't have shit without Grace. She's the one that did all the real work. And she was my friend first, remember? Or Trima, and I brought you them. And not to mention, the fucking irony of Mr. Peace going fucking Visigoth on his friend. Has that occurred to you, you lousy hypocrite?"

"Milan, I was trying to clear the way. Don't you see, I had to do something... You stole my woman, son."

He squints. "Now we're even? It's all okay? Is that what you're saying?"

"More or less."

"This is what happens when you mess around with things like peace. You get trouble. Real trouble." A crimson pool collects on his nostril, splashes to the ground. "You don't love her. You say you love her, but she doesn't feel it. What good is it? Sorry, Bob... I can't promise you anything."

"Could you at least not mention this incident to Elena... I mean... unless you decide to break up..."

I can't parse his glare.

These nights the most brilliant light in the city is a memorial. Luminous blue tubes shooting up from scarred earth into the heavens. Depending on the night and where you are, the atmospheric conditions, they will appear as beacon, bat-signal, searchlight, ET attractor, awesome thing of beauty, very American, affirmative, sad as hell, haunted, haunting, a collective continual grieving. A lamp lit at the altar. Tonight the outlines of the beams are crisp, there's a clean oval where light touches cloud. I can see spirits whirling around, using the brightness as a portal for dimensional travel, souls released into the afterlife. (Because if life doesn't go on forever and ever, then it never was to begin with, right? I mean, it would be truly pointless.)

I'm taking my time getting home; I am almost certain that Milan was on his way to see Elena (wherever it is they meet). I am also almost certain that he will tell her of my admittedly primitive behavior. Who knows? Perhaps she will understand my actions for what they are, driven by love and desperation. But I'm not confident, especially since the weasel scored a good red badge with his nose, which was puffing up even before he left me. I in fact took the worse beating, and I'm not sure whether that works for me or against. I get my cell and call home. I'm praying for the machine. "Hello?" Elena says.

I can't think of what to say. We have caller ID, so she's willing to talk to me. "Hello, Elena."

"Where are you?"

"Down the street."

"Let's meet somewhere."

"Alright." I don't like how this is playing out. "Where?"

"Whatever. Parachute?"

"I'm right there now. Sure... Elena, you don't want me to come home?"

"Be there in five." She hangs up.

I open the door to the café, a cozy warmth engulfing me. The front smoking room is tiny, especially when the doors to the sidewalk seats are closed. Bouncy horn-driven jazz plays low on the sound-system, no laptops, two readers, four couples, and a free table. I get a piece of chocolate cake and a double espresso and sit down at the table, stirring in three packets of sugar. I'm facing one of the readers, a middle-aged, rapidly balding man, leaned over his slim paperback. He turns a page, takes a long drag off his cigarette, then slowly exhales as he reads the next page, and so on. He stubs the cigarette out finally and looks up at me staring at him. I look away, but I can see peripherally that he's scrutinizing me. I look back and he is now holding the volume up so that I will see what it is: Camus' *The Stranger*. Parachute is just the sort of place a grown man would come and publicly read Camus in a misguided effort to pick up college kids. But why does he want me to see it? I read it years ago, and only remember that someone kills an Arab, and something about a mother's funeral. Maybe without the bandana, and downtown, my badass Latino self reads like off-the-boat Arab. Then what the hell does he mean flashing me that cover? A threat? Some kinky come on? I turn away again, looking to the door just as Elena opens it, letting in a blast of cold night air. A few steps behind her is the weasel, a bandage over his nose, his eye swollen and violet. They don't seem in good spirits as they sit down, business-like. Neither takes off their coat. "You have to order at the counter," I say.

"It's okay," Elena says. The weasel says nothing, his bruised face otherwise a blank.

"Let me explain."

"No, Bob. There's no need. You..." and her calm seems to crumble as she looks at Milan's banged up face with horror. "You went past explanations when you attacked him."

"It wasn't like that. I only planned on speaking to him. Then something took over. I lost control, I know. Milan," I turn pointedly to address him. "I'm sorry for what happened. You know that."

He stares down at the table, stays silent.

Elena takes a deep breath, actively restabilizing. "Well, you'll understand that you losing control like that would be of some concern to me, living under the same roof."

"Elena, I'm not dangerous. Come on. It's me. Bob. Not dangerous... Hey, he definitely nailed me worse, anyway. Milan, tell her you beat me up worse."

"I hit him," Milan mumbles.

"See? Fight. Between friends. I started it, yes, but he fought, too. Between men. We were communicating."

"It's not the point, Bob," says Elena. "You crossed the line. You're unstable. And I can't deal any more. Understand?"

"Unstable?" I shout to the alarm of Mr. Camus. "I'm a rock."

The new lovers share a private glance, agreeing on their planned course of action with the volatile lunatic. I'm not surprised that Elena's tone sounds completely alien, like the soothing voices on airplanes, like therapists, phone-sex girls. "Bob, there's no point in arguing. You live however you want to. I mean, it's your life, after all. But I've had enough. So, I would like you to have your things out of the apartment by tomorrow."

"What? Why? Come on. I know I made a mistake. I see that now. I get it that we have no future. It's painful, but I can accept it over time..."

"Bob," she says, calmly, "I need you to leave. *I* need *you* to leave."

"Listen to her," says Milan.

"Elena, you know my situation. Where the hell am I supposed to go?"

"You can move your things into storage. There's a place four blocks away." The easy preparedness of her answer hurts.

"One day's notice?"

Now she can't look at me. She stares at her knuckles. Milan covers her hand with his, giving it a reassuring squeeze. "Don't you see she's brittle?" Milan says.

"Shut the fuck up, man."

"Bob!" she says.

"Yes, I see it, Milan. I've seen it before, I've seen many versions of it. Many times over."

"Then, just do as she asks..." He rubs her pinkie with his thumb and I see her take succor from the act like a tired child arriving home. He leans his face into her scalp. I remember her floral oily smell. The way her long lashes look when she's asleep. The rough undersides of her dancer's feet. All gone. Kaput. She turns to face me, she has a small smile. "Listen, if you want me to help find you a place, or some other help, we can work that out. We can figure out a friendship later. But you must move out now. I won't go back until tomorrow night. Please, Bob. I'm trying to do this in a good way."

"What do you mean help?" I say. "What kind of help? Look, punching out your so-called best friend when he fucks your so-called sweetie is not crazy. It's almost a moral obligation, for Chrissakes! Besides, nobody was badly hurt. No great damage done. No hospitalization. And missy, I wouldn't get on my high horse, when you're still willing to fuck me!" The couple at the adjacent table stop flipping through the newspaper. Camus looks up, clearly intrigued. I lower my voice, and I notice Camus subtly tipping his head in our direction. "Or do you need help too, Elena?"

"Yes," she says quietly, to my surprise. "I'm getting it... and it allowed me to notice a few patterns clearly."

I turn to Milan to see whether my news has had any effect. He's staring at my chocolate cake. "She told me," he says. "I know about it. Difficult time."

That's it? She's figured it out and I lose. It's very simple. They're together. I move. Those are the terms of the defeat, my surrender. I have no choice but to accept. To the winner, the spoils! The electricity between them is undeniable, the charge finally cutting through the layers of my resentment, showing me the true face of their affection. How I hate to see it, the bubble of energy containing the two lovebirds, feeding them. I remember being there with her once. Now it is expulsion, desolation, toil. No tenderness, no friendship, no acceptance, no boom-boom. Bob cut loose, singular in the ocean like poor Pip in *Moby Dick*. I feel dizzy, imagining my feet touching the ground, the ground covering the earth's surface, and space all around me extending out infinitely. All locations are temporary. The thought expands in my mind.

"Okay," I say. "I'll clear out by tomorrow. I'll mail you the keys."

"Fine," says Elena.

"Good," says Milan. They both get up, and without another word, exit. I see Camus follow them with his eyes, grinning very much like a man who has overheard juicy dish. His book lies closed in front of him. "Hey!" I say. "Yes, you! Do you know how evil it is to take pleasure in someone else's misery?"

"Excuse me?" says Camus.

"You know what I mean. Don't pretend. And also, did no one inform you that reading Camus in a smoky downtown café is pathetic to begin with and completely unacceptable in any man over the age of twenty-two?"

"What?" says the bewildered Camus.

"Good evening, Monsieur!" I say, knocking down my tepid sweet espresso, and storming outside. I was hoping that setting Camus straight would release some energy, settle my trepidation, but the world seems all edges. Full of forces ready to tear me to shreds. Dissolve me into atoms. The cutie kids walking around feel out of sync, and the yellow cabs glide by, hissing, sinister. Woe! Woe! Woe is me! I have been thrown out again into this lousy life! Another dream torn down! No choice! Got to go home now! Got to pack it up!

The pathos of the cardboard box. The fact that I never threw out the ones I moved in with must mean something. I just have to tape them up and they're good as new. Two suitcases and eight boxes. Finding no place to settle is the banal dilemma of the global citizen, but each so-called home is invested with sentiment, relationships, curiosities, energy, each floater identity is good for its time, is believed in fully as an act of faith, I suppose. Even if we can't ultimately know each other, we can at least pretend well, keeping an ideal in mind. (Perhaps to know more than each other, beyond each other, to know what is true, what is eternal?) A battered cardboard box, filled with socks, belts, ties, and "KITCHEN" scrawled on it in red magic-marker: my life. I can't afford too much sentiment. I close it, tape it up, and speed-dial Grace.

"Yes?"

"Elena gave me the boot."

"Oh."

"I'm supposed to clear out by tomorrow."

"I see."

"Fucking Milan."

"He says you attack him."

"Oh great! He's already called you! Weasel! Total weasel!"

"He call because he concerned... About you, Bob."

"Oh hell! Hell! He's not concerned about me, Grace! Don't you see? I'm kicked out! He's with Elena! Those happen to be the facts!"

"Please calm down."

She's right. I quietly take a few abdominal breaths. "Listen. It's true, we had a slight altercation that I initiated. It was a mistake. I know it."

"This is what I say."

"What say?"

"Satan."

"What? This is Satan, now?"

"Once you make a deal, Satan take over. Make you violent, Bob. Maybe we should stop messing with peace."

"Asshole Milan. He gave you his don't mess with peace voodoo bullshit! Watch out, peace will get you! Be afraid, be very afraid of peace. Oooh, look out, peace is pissed off…" I grab my shirts and toss them in another box, hangers and all.

"We can end it, Bob. There is a way."

"No, Grace. We're right there! Not now!"

"We even make our money back."

"Money back? What are you talking about?"

"There is a way. You'll see."

"Grace, I am in no shape for your cryptic shit! What the hell is going on?!... Grace?... Grace?..."

"Don't shout."

"Sorry... What way?"

"You want to stay over here for couple of days?"

"Well, sure. Thanks." She is both kind and clever because the question of staying longer is already answered. Nonetheless, it gives me a place to take my things. "How about I come by in the late morning?"

"Come over. I show you the way out. Big time."

"Alright. Thanks again," I say and hang up. She said we would get our money back, which at the moment would certainly be good. I only hope she hasn't committed to some scam-artist. Besides, we're a craze in Amsterdam, dammit!

Like a robot, I empty my drawers, pull books off my shelves. I don't have the heart to go hunting for my books that might have strayed into hers. I take my files from the cabinet, pulling out the Peace INC. folder. I've kept my favorite print-outs with the idea of starting a scrap book. I look at the earliest images that came back to us: four Albanians outside their consulate under an umbrella; a group of Pakistani students, holding banners, surrounded by German police; a freckled teenager in London at a peace demo with a zonked smile; then a series from the clubs after the peaceholes hit, blurry, trippy, girls and boys; articles about Equarius; and most recently a curious anonymous posting of someone in our T-shirt (looks male, but can't be sure), half-running across a street. It was marked Jerusalem; I tried to follow-up, the party hasn't answered. I realize in the big scheme of things, none of this amounts to much, but looking through the photos—the earnestness in the Pakistani girl's eyes, the plainness of the Brit boy's smile, the blur that might or might not be from Jerusalem—makes me feel good. And those trippy club kids? Why not? At least they're happy temporarily. Beats killing and torturing each other. I look at the images with an unfamiliar type of pride, realizing it's the worst moment to abandon Peace INC., just when it's blossoming. Watching the Terror Channel last night, with its lists of terrorists and plots worldwide, and footage of bodies piling up, of deadly gases and viruses missing and smuggled, I was happy to be doing Peace INC. I'm able to honor the boy I used to be, the young fella who lost his world so rudely. I put the file in the box and tape it up. I try not to look too closely at Elena's things, as I strip and crawl naked into our bed one last time.

I call Grace from the sidewalk where the car service van drops me off with my stuff. A minute later Mr. Tae Kwon Do walks bowlegged, down the stairs. The morning once again promises summer, barely eleven and it must be in the seventies. Tinny Greek music drifts out from the diner. "Let me help you," he says. "Tommy," he says, offering me his death-grip. I shake his hand, quickly disengaging. "Yes. We've met," I say. "Thank you."

He bends at the knees, grabbing two stacked boxes of books. He straightens effortlessly, picks up a suitcase with his left hand, and makes his way steadily through the court-yard and up the stairs. I also pick up two boxes (one being the super-light, socks, ties, and belts box) and follow him into the apartment. He puts the things down and immediately turns for the next load. "Hello," I say, but there's no reply. The door to the bedroom is closed. I run down and pass Tommy on the steps coming up with an even larger load (three boxes stacked and a garbage bag!). I run two smaller loads quickly and we're done. I shut the door, go directly into the office, and wait. Tommy comes in with two glasses of water. "Not so bad," he says, surveying my possessions.

That could mean far too many things for me to even think about in my current state. I sip the cool water. "Good," I say. "Thanks for the hand."

"No big deal." He sips from his glass, improbably flexing his bicep in the act.

We're quiet for a bit. "Where's Grace?" I ask.

"Oh, she's in the bedroom." He blinks absently.

"Is there a problem?"

"Well, I wanted to say some things. And, well, actually, she didn't think I should. So we argued about that..."

"Hey!" He seemed to be drifting into another story. "What kind of things? About the business? About the sale?"

"No. No. Now I see you, I think she's probably right, it's stupid."

"Just say it."

"Well, you know Grace is my fiancé."

"What? I thought you were her cousin. Her self-appointed consigliere."

"Third cousin, actually fourth. Mostly I'm her fiancé."

"Well, isn't everyone full of surprises."

"So, she talks to me. You know? She tells me things. And she tells me... you might have fallen prey to Satan."

"Oh, come on! Tommy! Give me a break, huh?"

"Bob, let me finish. I respect Grace's beliefs... but I'm no holy roller. You know? To me it just means in her own way she thinks you might be a problem. Now, seeing you, I don't think you will turn into a problem. But I wanted to go on record. Right?" To his credit, he keeps very still, avoiding any swagger.

"Noted. I don't plan on causing problems."

He nods and goes back into the bedroom. A second later, Grace comes out into the office. "Sorry about that. He blow what I say all out of proportion. But that's how he is. He's a good guy, but dense." She taps the side of her head and laughs in a doting way. "Now," she says. "Look at this." She hands me a stack of e-mail print-outs. I flip through them quickly; correspondence back and forth from Equarius in the last week. "Look at first one," she says smiling.

hi guys,

as you know the sales are going great. and since the shipments were enlarging we thought that you could save on shipping and have them mail directly to us.

peace out,

charlotte

"Wait a minute..." I say.

"Keep going," she says.

Dear Charlotte,

For the moment we would like to keep matters status quo. Thank you for the concern.

Best wishes,

Peace INC.

"Excellent!" I say. "Grace, you're one sharp cookie! Those club-kid entrepreneurs were trying to cut us out!"

"You bet. Read on."

hi guys,

some very exciting news from this side. and we've had a few inquiries regarding your peace logo. you have it registered and everything, right? let us know if you're interested in us setting something up.

peace out,

charlotte

"Outrageous!" I say. She raises her chin, inciting me to go on.

Dear Charlotte,

Yes, the logo is registered and overseen by a team of lawyers.

But we are delighted there is interest. We would be happy to talk licensing and/or fees depending on the project.

Best wishes,

Peace INC.

"Grace, superb! But I..."

"Oh shush. Did you have the mind to think about these kind of things? Anyway, it doesn't take Einstein. I ask you when necessary. Like now. See, is serious, they capitalizing sentence." She hands me a sheet.

Hi Guys,

This is like totally informal, but we were talking over here and realized that we could take something you've started, and expand on it in many creative ways. The website, merchandising, we think we are in a very good position to take Peace INC., to the next level. Now, of course, that may not interest you, which is why we make this informal inquiry. We were thinking of something in the range of $60,000 (U.S.) for the whole operation, website, all trademarks, contacts? If this sounds interesting we will have our lawyers contact you.

peace out,

Charlotte

"Well?" says Grace.

"Interesting. Very interesting." And I do find it so, because sixty grand will cover company debts with ten large left over. It would allow me to find my own apartment (albeit still in personal debt, but, hey, who isn't these days?). "I don't know, Grace. It's off, somehow."

"We wash our hands. Finished. Then whatever happen, happen. See?"

"Simply purify. Ask for forgiveness. I get it. Satan took it, so cut it loose... But don't you defeat your purpose? I mean by selling to these guys? They're the ones who will exploit the most Satanic elements. Then, something you created, I created, we created, will be turned into a monstrosity of neo-ET-club-chic frou-frou. This is the true test, Grace! The test of faith. Do we just sell our child to the first slave merchant? Simply because our baby is spirited and a drain on our resources? Peace INC., is maturing rapidly, Grace. And we can steer it through its turbulent adolescence. Get it back on track! Get the message right!"

She's massaging her temple like she has a headache. I decide to knock it off. We're dead quiet for many minutes. "I see your point," Grace says.

"Meaning?"

"We stick it out."

Now I'm not sure whether we should take the money and forget about it. And do what exactly? Where exactly?

"Excellent! We stick it out! Okay," I say, and spin in my chair to the keyboard. I prepare to send an e-mail to Charlotte. "With your permission." With great pomp, I crack my knuckles.

"Please," she says, bowing and smiling coyly like a stage geisha.

Dear Charlotte,

My oh my! Your offer sure took us by surprise! Well, we greeted it with many feelings, including excitement, pride, and happiness. We want to know some more from you guys, as informally as you want to make it. More than a lump sum, how about a larger talk about percentages and opportunities? Also, what are your plans to expand, so we have a notion? Hear from you soon, and, ciao!

Best Wishes

Peace INC.,

Grace laughs, reading over my shoulder. "You messing with her, right?"

"A little. I don't know," I say hitting the send button. "Just want to see what they're made of. We forge forward then... One of Iqbal's customers writes for Time Out... He says he's interested... And we expand our... our... outreach! Contact our primary list again. Get the religious and politicos all heated up! The Mideast is on fire! War everywhere! World's gone berserk! We're in excellent position. We can make a difference, Grace."

"Only difference is when people wake up," she says, standing, wiggling her handless sleeves, before going back to the bedroom and shutting the door. I might just be paranoid, but her comment seemed pointed, like I was being reprimanded. Was my pitch too strong?

CHAPTER VIII

t's hot and muggy and baby Devi is revved up, zoom-ing effortlessly out of her highchair and into the living room, throwing anything she can get her hands on onto the floor. I must be quick, chasing after her, swooping her up by the tiny waist of her dress. "Noooo," she protests, legs kicking, fists flailing, as we make our way back to the kitchen.

"Yes," I say calmly. "We have to have our breakfast. Let Uncle Bob at least have his coffee. Please, sweetie," I say as softly as possible, setting her back on her perch. Her mouth is decidedly in an unhappy frown, but her cheeks are flushed, her brown cherubic curls all-too-cute, her eyes lit like diamonds. Baby Devi folds her arms as if she's a granny resigned to her fate, and that too is nearly unbear-able to witness. "Thank you, sweetie-pie," I say, as she allows me to swing the tabletop in front of her. "Now," I say, pouring myself a coffee, taking the first life-affirming sip, "a little apple juice." I pour two glasses halfway, and set hers down without fuss. I go to the stove and stir the mush, a certain "mix of oats and grains" that is said to be a particularly good breakfast for baby girls. I pour some more water into the "mix" to avoid the congealing I suffered in my first effort.

When Anna heard I'd been kicked out, she called with news of her own. I don't know why it surprised me Milan'd moved out too, asking for a divorce. I also don't know why that obvious possibility hurt so much when it became real. Owarama! Man, it hurt! And made worse by the fact that Anna didn't hate him, didn't dislike him. She even said she still loved him as the father of their daughter. Understandable, I suppose. Nonetheless irritating, since it made it very awkward to vent my rage to the one person who should sympathize. Anna had no bile for anybody. Not Milan, not Elena, not me. She was only hurt, and slightly bewildered at the drastic change. Milan would continue to support the household (most likely touching Elena's fortune!), until they could make the formal arrangements in the divorce.

So Anna's big problem was how she was going to look for a job and pay for (much less trust) day care. My big problem was I had to leave Grace's the next day. When I pointed out the obvious intersection of these two vectors of need, Anna laughed with surprising gusto. Her initial response was indulging the fantasy as perverse revenge. But I persisted in pointing out that though a bit weird, it actually made sense. Milan would hate it, she said, and then she was quiet on the other end for a very long time, before she sighed, Oh why not? Three nights, four days, and counting, while Anna temps for an agency owned by one of her oldest friends. So, couch-to-couch pour moi!

I stir the viscous brew one last time, empty the contents into a Daisy Duck bowl, scraping the wooden ladle clean of mush with my forefinger. I open the jar of honey and pour out a nice spiral, topping it off with Rice Milk. It looks beautiful, though no question, it does taste like a two-by-four. Poor baby Devi. "Here you go, honey." I set the bowl down in front of her, tucking in a bright red spoon. Her face is still concentrated in a defiant pout, the lower lip now proudly showing its disdain for the mush, this travesty she is subjected to without any regard for her humanity. She looks at it and then accusingly at me. She says nothing, but her gaze exposes my hypocrisy, challenges my inability to stand by the mush. I realize as I approach her the challenge is one I cannot ultimately win. She knows the mush is bad. She knows I know it's bad. Hopelessly, I take a mini spoonful, and make a big drama of eating it. "Yumyum," I say unconvincingly, and as I do some mush lodges in the back of my throat and I cough. I look over at baby Devi and she's giggling, rocking back and forth, clapping.

"Ahem," I say, drinking some apple juice. "Alright, alright. It tastes lousy."

"Yay!" More clapping.

"But you know you still have to eat it."

She turns the bowl so the spoon faces her. She takes a mouthful, frowning. "Yuk. Tell Mommy you hate it," she says, before puckering up her face for another mouthful. She slowly works herself into a steady disciplined effort to do away with the mush. She's a pretty cool three-year-old.

Turning suddenly into a surrogate daddy is bizarre. You're walking the dark woods, and what path there is splits into two equally thick and obscure groves. You pick one. Or is one picked for you? How would you know the difference? But you want to believe things add up somehow, that there is a larger purpose to all the mayhem. At each juncture you incorporate the random event into a story of your always imminent redemption. Yesterday night, not yet asleep on the couch, I listened to Anna explaining to a cranky baby Devi that daddy was staying at a friend's house. When baby Devi followed up with her predictable (and quite reasonable) "Why?" Anna paused for many moments before answering, "For fun, bunny." Maybe it was my imagination, but I heard in Anna's voice what Milan said he loved, the deep confidence, even under great duress. She was not waiting to be saved by anything.

I must be careful not to fall for this baby. I've never experienced such attenuated tenderness, the funny flutter in the heart. Devi is not my child, yet her newness, her wonder, her button nose and milk-tooth smile, her mini body, toes and fingers, her precocious words and reckless relationship to things, all these make it difficult for me to keep the requisite emotional distance. I must not get pulled in by her life! She is, after all, Milan's child. He is her father. He will come on the weekend to pick her up, for example. Anna tells me he was furious I'd moved in, and said some very damaging things she wouldn't repeat. Of course, he was too compromised to be able to object further. He even offered to pay for daycare, but Anna insisted on our arrangement after she saw how easily baby Devi took to me (it also let her feel confident the care was to her specifications). Milan didn't have a leg to stand on, and feeling good about his impotent rage was my great consolation.

Yes, let him envy the time I spend with his delightful child. He knows me well enough to know I'll be responsible, although I think he said the opposite to Anna. I'm sure it heightens the ache of realizing what he's lost, to feel that I have easier access to a secret place in his heart than he does. Well, the idiot deserves it.

"All done," says baby Devi, hands up like she's won a race. There's a ring of mush on her cheeks. "Excellent!" I say and grab a handywipe to tidy her up. "Thanks, honey." I pull the table back and she steps down carefully and runs into the living room. She climbs up on the couch, jumping up and down.

"Sweetie. Come on, let's get off there." I grab her and we both sit cross-legged on the carpet on either side of the multi-colored Playskool farm. I yank the string. "The duck goes quack," says the voice.

"*Totoro!*" she says.

"We've seen *Totoro* an awful number of times."

"So?"

"So, it gets boring, don't you think?"

"Why?"

"Well, it's the same. We know what happens." Actually, all I remember from the animé is a giant furry cat that's also a bus.

Her outsized eyes look up from under her focused brows. The pout is threatening a comeback. "You do the same things again and again," she says. Her tone is petulant, but she is definitely making an argument that is deep and uncanny enough for me to get *Totoro* and pop it in the

DVD. "Where's Daddy?" she says as I hit play. She hasn't asked since two days ago.

"He's coming the day after tomorrow, sweetie. Tomorrow and just one more. You know he had to go away." So far, we've left it at that and though she is never happy with the answer, she's cooperative. *Totoro* begins and she gives over to its familiar hypnotism, but her face is still troubled, like there's a mystery whose solution she dreads. "I'll be right in the kitchen, Devi. I'm going to check in with my office, okay?" She nods, samurai-style. "Okay," I say and speed-dial Grace. The loud fan blows in a warm breeze. The kitchen is drenched in yellow morning light.

"Hello, Peace INC.," Grace says chirpily.

"You got any more of what you're taking?"

"Sure, Bob. Called life."

"Really, now. What gives?"

"We got a good order today from Tokyo. Hundred T-shirts and..."

"Hey, great! And... ?"

"Two carton condoms." She laughs like a sixth grader.

"Alright! Largest condom order yet! I told you there was something there. The Japanese, yes, of course."

"College peace group, NPLP."

"Excellent! So... I gather no further response from those thieving neo-tribals?"

"No, not from them. But we get call today from a strange man."

"He have a name?"

"Funny name. Nyal. Spell N-J-A-L. Njal. From Iceland."

"And what does this Njal want?"

"He want to meet with us."

"He say why?"

"He says he's a big fan... he want to share visions."

"Sounds like a fruitcake."

"He also says he make us rich."

"And what do you think about that, Grace?"

"We should see who he is. Right?"

"Absolutely!" Ho ho! I knew when those rats at Equarius made an offer there was something else brewing. I could smell it. I'm also aware that things cost a lot in Iceland, and rich has to mean a bit more than sixty grand! "Set it up, Grace, by all means. Tonight!"

Njal said to Grace that we should look for a man in a bunny outfit. She thought that's what he said. Well, there are no giant rabbits at Xeno, though it is surprisingly crowded for so early. Iqbal is alone behind the bar, harried. "'Sup, man?" I say. We bang fists.

"New policy. Happy hour. Don't I look happy?" His movements pouring, shaking, stirring, tapping, wiping, changing, are a blur as he takes care of the rush, before coming back and leaning exhausted against the bar. "Hel-lo," he says to Grace.

"Hi," she says with something like coyness in her voice.

"So," I say, "Have you seen a man in a bunny outfit?"

He smiles. "What's it worth to you?"

"We will be forever grateful," says Grace kittenishly.

"From you," Iqbal says, leaning towards her, "I guess that's enough. You're lucky I'm observant. As a matter of fact, there was this guy who got a Tanquery-martini about twenty minutes ago. Went in the back room."

"He was in a bunny outfit?" I ask.

"Well... yeah. I noticed his shirt was unusual. The pattern when you looked closely was entirely made up of bunnies all huddled together."

"I told you! Bunnies!" says Grace.

"Astonishing," I say. "Iqbal, you the man. The main man."

Shying away from the compliment, he quickly fixes us both Ketel One martinis. Grace, who ordinarily can't be coerced into doing anything, takes her drink with a squirmy protest. We gently walk our drinks up the steps to the back room, and go to the only table with a single man, whose shirt, on closer inspection, is crawling with bunnies. "Njal?" I say, rousing him from a trance. He gets up languorously, and gestures for us to set our drinks down. "Njal," he says offering me his cool hand.

"Bob," I say. "Grace." They shake too and we all sit down.

"Nice place. I like it." he says smiling. His accent is public-school British with some Hawaiian surfer thrown in. He's quite a cutie himself in a slightly androgynous way. His features are delicate, fingers long but fleshy, full lips and cheeks still holding some babyfat. The 70s teen runaway hairdo completes the artful gamin.

"So you know a little about us, Njal. What's your deal?"

He leans back and crosses his ankle over his knee, grinning big like a rock star. "Well, at the moment I'm kind of a rock star." Ah ha!

"Really?" says Grace.

He takes a moment to consider his answer. "Yes," he laughs, "At the moment, I would say that it seems to be the case. Yes, coming soon to a music store near you. Njal's Saga."

"That's your band?" I ask.

"Yeah..." he says, taken momentarily by a private drama, staring at the table. "That's my band. So, it's like my saga, understand?" He laughs at this, and I can do no better than smile neutrally. "Named after the most famous Icelandic epic. You know it?"

"Sure," I say. "Njal's Saga. I know the name. And..."

"Doesn't matter. We had a different idea when we started anyway. The whole thing evolved, understand? The music, the sound, the message. Four years ago, when we were much younger, we had a different idea. You know, explore the darkness, you know, illuminate the shadows. So, yah, we still made danceable music, but it was pretty noisy, you know, lots of samples, and street, and industrial stuff. It was filled with a kind of rage, you know, because of what is happening on the planet. Songs like "Bad Blood" and "Shit the Rich" and "Time to Die." We had a few hits in Europe. Some club hits. Radio play in the U.K., France, Italy. Some good stuff. But finally we burned ourselves out, you understand? In every way, totally burned out. So, yah, we broke up kind of. And those with substance problems went into programs, and the rest, five total, all went in some funny direction. One day I met Jon, the lead guitarist, at a party and we started talking exactly on the same wavelength, you understand? Exactly. Connecting. So we decided to contact everyone and, amazingly, we all seem to have gone through a similar process..."

"So, you're back together. And that has something to do with Peace INC.?" I say.

"I'm sorry," Njal says. "I'd only like you to know how it was I found you. Yes, Njal's Saga reunited!" He slaps the table. "We realized that all of us wanted to get beyond where we're stuck. You know, oh this sucks and that sucks and poor me, poor broken-hearted me. Always looking at the past, not the future. Negative is easy... We would take the radical step to the positive."

"Meaning?" asks Grace sensibly.

"Well," says Njal, like a drowsy prince. "We were trying to figure that out when I came upon your website and the peace logo. It was like a sign, understand? We worked the first track in a whole new approach... 'Peace for the Children'."

"Wow!" I say. "How interesting. That's great, Njal, really great. That you were inspired by our work. "Peace for the Children," huh? It sounds... well... it's interesting."

Njal laughs impishly. "You said interesting not once, but twice. Yes, that's exactly the point. Makes your skin crawl to even imagine a song called 'Peace for the Children'. Why is that? The first time I proposed it, the drummer nearly barfed. Then we sat there for days and got deeper and deeper into the idea until we all felt it, you know? What it means to want peace for children. We rented a cottage in Berne, the most boring place on the planet, and worked and worked on it until it shined... And it does shine."

"You want to license the logo?" asks Grace.

"Well, yes... Actually, we would be interested in buying the whole business. Lock, stock and barrel."

"Did you talk with Charlotte?" I ask. "In Amsterdam?"

Njal tilts his head to the side, smiles. "Alright, busted. Yah, I did try to arrange the buy through Equarius. Save the hassle."

"So you see T-shirts first," says Grace. "In magazines or some place."

"Yes," Njal says. "In fact we worked your peace sign into the whole concept, understand? ... It would give our comeback a clear message."

"What does rich mean to you?" I ask.

"Very good," Njal says, gingerly applauding. "Very good. Well, we said sixty before. Let's say a hundred."

I turn to Grace and her indecipherable mask is back. The way she regards Njal makes me suspect she is seeing Satan again. "Well, what do you say, Grace?"

"I think we discuss privately."

"Well, sure," says Njal. He reaches under the table and produces a black plastic DVD box. "Look at it. Then you decide. You'll see that we have much in common."

"Okay," Grace says, taking the box. "Nice to meet you, Njal." She stands up, and looks at me to follow. I'd wanted to stay, and get a better feeling for the guy, but now it's too complicated. I knock down my drink, and get up too. "We'll talk soon," I say, shaking hands.

"Sure," says Njal, gazing at his empty glass.

I follow Grace as she waves to Iqbal and makes her way quickly outside. "Peace, brother," I say to Iqbal, who flashes me the sign in response. Grace is halfway up the block when I come out into the torpid night air. "Hey!" I yell, "Wait up!" I run to catch her, weaving through groups of young revelers. "So?" I say, keeping up with her very fast clip.

"I don't like it. Why he lie to us? That's no good."

"Well, yeah. But, you know, he wanted to sell us..."

"Still. They trying to cash in on the whole club drug scene. He try to play it down. I don't like it, Bob."

"I see what you mean. Sure. I mean, maybe. We should at least look at the DVD, no?"

She holds up the black box, glaring at it. "Why?"

"Taxi!" I yell, finger out. Grace raises her eyebrow at the extravagance. "Grace," I say, "A hundred grand on the table! Hundo, baby! Hundo! Hundo!" She sighs, managing a wan smile.

A children's choir chants "Peace," and again, staccato, "Peace," the high synchronized voices resonating in a large space. At the third chant, "Peace," there's a flash of an all white children's choir, then "Peace," and an all black children's choir. "Peace," again it has become a pulse, and a flash of what I think is an all-Mexican children's choir. There's a low techno twitter, a rich colorful pastoral chord, then another. "Peace," an East Asian choir; "Peace," Middle Eastern; the chant stays steady going from child choir to child choir as the chords give way to a slapping baseline. "Peace," sounding like all the choruses mixed, "Peace." And then bam! there's our sign! More kids! Sign! Kids! Sign! "Alright!" I say, turning to Grace, who's showing no feeling at all.

"Alright!" shouts baby Devi, throwing her fist up. She's sitting in Anna's lap and mommy joins in with her own imitation of Devi's "Alright!" Anna leans over and pats my shoulder. I turn to see her beaming with excitement. The groove builds to all-out wildness. These Icelanders got it going on! The images switch to children: running, playing, laughing, all colors, all sizes, and the chorus switches to "For the Children..." also declared like an anthem. Then "Peace," in counterpoint. Both phrases taken through echo chambers and sound loops, child voices stretching and morphing into ominous basso and pure texture. Clips of kids swimming, flying kites, riding bikes, going to school, eating lunch, making faces. All nicely cut to beats, the peace sign a coruscating refrain. Very danceable, I'm thinking, when baby Devi jumps from her mother's lap, starts twisting side to side, kicking her right leg out, waving her arms in the air, completely getting down! "Get down!" I say. "Go, baby Devi, go!" Which I shouldn't have done, because she becomes self-conscious and goes running back to her mommy's lap. Nonetheless, it has passed the baby-boogie test with flying colors.

The song thins out its layers to a basic baseline, a scratchy violin, and the voices, but they are joined by gospel singers souping up the words. (If you're dancing, you keep moving, but feel like you're holding your breath.) The clips are more structured now, footage from everywhere, of kids marching, smiling, high-school bands, military academies, scouts, sports teams. American, South American, African, Caribbean, German, English, Japanese, Soviet, French, Chinese, Indian, children of all ages and sizes, from all time since film existed, democratic children, fascist children, racist children, left-wing children, fundamentalist children, children of every faith and ethnicity, marching in one direction or another. At first you try to guess who they are or what they are or from when they are until the rhythm speeds up and the rows of marching children are no more than colorful movement on the screen. The instruments all die out leaving only the choir voices singing the entire phrase once, the screen black, and echoing space between the words.

"Yay!" says baby Devi, clapping. "Yay!" Anna joins in.

"Well..." I say, waiting on Grace... "That was something."

"I liked it," says Anna. "And so did big-girl Devi. Didn't you, bunny?" She puts her face into Devi's belly, making her squeak with laughter.

"Grace?" I say. She's barely rocking back and forth, her hands cupped in her lap like a meditator. A tear rolls down the side of her face. "It's good," she says. "The message will reach many." She casually wipes the tear away with her sleeve.

"Pretty funky," I say. I'm of course relieved that Grace is moved by it, but I'm not exactly clear what the message is. "What do you think it means?" I ask Anna.

"First of all, the song itself is lively. You know? And the clips are great. What does it mean? Who knows? All sorts of things. Everything you learn as a child is a kind of indoctrination, I guess. I mean, that's what I try to do with Devi, right? I can't help it. I teach her what she needs to know to survive. How not to get hurt. How can I stop giving her my culture, whatever that is, my values? What's the alternative?

Let them go wild?" Anna stops herself, smiling at the realization that she wasn't exactly sure what the video meant.

"And are they saying that Nazi kids and Jihadi kids and Thanksgiving Parade kids are all the same somehow, because they happen to be marching?" I ask.

"No, not like that," says Grace. "Message is simple. You must become innocent like a child. See face of the child? Full of trust. Full of love. Even if you make them march. Even when they get filled with hate. Their face full of faith... Plus, song totally rocks." She smiles, toothy.

"So... you're fine with the sale?" I ask.

She nods yes. "Also, you know, our protection isn't all that special. We registered, but I talk to lawyer and he say it would cost money to fight it. If someone steal it."

"What?!... Okay, okay... If you're happy to sell, Grace, then we'll figure out the terms with lawyers. We should find out how high they're willing to go."

"We got no money for lawyers."

"Don't worry. I'll sort that out. Me business, remember?" I point to my chest.

"I like the message of Njal's Saga," Grace says, standing. "And hundred grand not too bad a payday."

"You bet," says Anna.

"Goodnight," says Grace. "Tomorrow." She points at me and steps over the pile of Legos (my attempted mansion) to get out the door.

"A hundred thousand," Anna says. "That's so good, Bob. How about a glass of wine to celebrate?'

"Well, there's nothing quite to celebrate yet... Sure, a hundred grand is excellent. You know, it's true, I did it for the money, but recently it's starting to feel like different. Like it's got some life of its own."

"Even better to celebrate."

"Why not? Let's do it! What do you say, baby, I mean, big-girl Devi?" I raise my hand for a high five. "Let's do it," she says slapping it. I pick her up and hold her on my hip. "I really liked your dancing, sweetie-pie," I say making her giggle and recoil with shyness.

Anna goes into the kitchen and comes back with a bottle of white and two glasses. "My glass!" Devi demands and Anna produces a baby plastic champagne glass, to her delight. She pours her a little grape juice, and us some wine. "Peace INC.," she says raising a toast. We clink glasses with each other, then tap Devi's. "To Devi's dance," I say. "Noooo," she says, holding the stem of her glass with both hands.

"Thanks for all the help, Bob," Anna says.

"Don't mention it. It's very good for me, anyway. And this one," I kiss Devi's rosy cheek, "is a delight. I should thank you."

"Anyway, you've been great, and..."

"Sure." We look into each other's eyes. Or at least I look into hers until she averts her gaze, and I cannot stop myself from staring dumbly at her painter-perfect Mogul lips. Her long, black hair is loose in ringlets, her cocoa skin dewy. "What?" she says.

"Sorry?"

"What's the look?" she asks smiling.

"Honestly?"

"Of course."

"You're very beautiful."

"Oh please," she says pushing a stray lock of hair off her face.

"You asked."

"Well, forget it."

"Forget what? You asked me a question. You know you are, anyway. I wasn't going anywhere with it."

"Don't." She polishes off her wine, and gets up, grabbing baby Devi. "Okay bunny, time to get ready for bed." She takes Devi into the bathroom and there is much squealing laughter, and chatter and water splashing. I get my bedroll and unfurl it on the couch. As soon as I lie down I am taken by a swirling panic that I just blew it with Anna and she'll ask me to leave just when there's not a dime to spare. And who knew they could just steal our logo? What if we can't fight it without money? Money! Money! Money! My heart starts to race, and then I hear Anna reading a bedtime story to Devi, the murmur so gentle, re-assuring, triggering thoughts of irretrievable security. I imagine myself a small boy being read to by his mother, being tucked into bed, kissed on the forehead, his face caressed. A sharp pain, a trapped cry, memory exploding in my heart, the warm smell of mother's neck, of father's after-shave mixed with smoke. Flashes of laughter around the dining table, father in his sleeveless T-shirt, humid air slowly warming the day. I am giving over to the warmth, trusting memory will calmly subside with time, a soft pink light fills my mind, returning me to now... I hear the door to the bedroom quietly shut, the lights go out. I smell Anna's faint perfume as she gets under the covers with me, her breath hot on my ear.

She was lonely. I was lonely. The whole damn world was lonely. We didn't have sex, but we made out like high-schoolers, held each other tight, and napped for a few hours. At some point, she got up and went to the bedroom to sleep with Devi. I drifted in and out of fitful dreams. The one that woke me permanently, terrifying in its dumb literal-ness: Anna and I on the very same couch having super-hot boom-boom! Seems my subconscious is pretty shallow. I saw dawn creep, heard the morning birds, the garbage trucks; I was agitated, but not at all guilty. Our make-out session was tender, sweet, full of easy release, and the plea-sure of simply being held. We weren't squirrelly having cof-fee, and before anything could be discussed, I promptly left (it's my day off from baby-sitting). Her smile was demure and friendly enough, as I stepped out.

I cannot afford confusion now. The sweetest hangover, the melancholy daydreaming of Anna's classic face, will have to wait. The questions will have to wait. Focus, baby, focus! Elena at first refused to meet me, she was so angry I'd moved in with Anna. Did I have any idea how difficult that was for Milan? Ha! I told her I had no choice, and I needed to talk to her in person. I suggested the Classic Garden, because we once shared a near-perfect afternoon there. She protested the location too, then agreed (still out of guilt, I suppose).

I go through the gate and down the grand steps, spy-ing four women in sleek white evening gowns posing in front of the big green lawn. There are special lights and tripods, assistants adjusting huge white screens like sails, and a ponytailed photographer actually in a crouch. I walk past the very French arcade of crab apples, deserted but for a pair of old wealthy ladies chatting on a bench ringed with fallen white and pink petals.

As I approach the Garden of the Muses (the lovely ladies frolic in the central fountain), I hear the one sound I decidedly do not want to hear: the cry of the weasel. I stay behind the hedges, getting closer to the source, and I hear Elena's stern tone, then the whimpering weasel, then Elena louder, wilder, the weasel now shouting, and I can make out the words, "You don't dictate how I should feel!"

And Elena, "Please. Let me handle it. God, you're driving me crazy."

And the weasel, "You don't know him. He's dangerous. And he's looking after my child, dammit!"

And Elena, kindly, heartbreakingly, "Trust me, dear one."

Well, enough of this crap! I turn the corner, prepared to take charge, when my eyes are assaulted by a hallucinogenic display of tulips. The garden is bursting red, yellow, orange, and violet, so dazzling the eye sees vibration, electricity. "Bob," says Milan approaching me.

"Milan," says Elena, following him.

"I got nothing to say to you," I say to him. His nose has healed pretty well, though underneath his eye is still purple.

"Why are you doing this, man? To get even with me? Huh? Is that why?"

Elena rightly grabs his arm, keeping our personal space intact. "Enough, Milan."

"Yes, Milan. Listen to your old lady."

"You're a real dickhead. And if you mess things up between Devi and me... I'll... I'll..."

"Milan!" scolds Elena.

"Milan, you need to talk to your wife, not to me, okay? Not to mention, jerko, you should be happy someone you trust instead of a questionable stranger is looking after baby Devi! I'm not the one who messed things up!"

He is momentarily shamed into a silence. Elena squeezes his arm. "Babka," she says quietly. "Let me talk to Bob alone, okay? We'll sort everything out."

Babka?! It takes a great deal of restraint not to sneer at the endearment as he nods and slowly walks away. "Some flowers, huh?" I say, smiling. I lead the way slowly to the fountain at the center, sitting on the carved stone edge. They've yet to turn the water on.

"Ten thousand tulips, I read in the paper." She spins once, taking in the brilliant spectacle. "They're incredible." She says it in a way that is all too familiar, brows raised, mouth downturned, as though the admission is coerced and painful. Like her sensitivity to beauty is so acute that acknowledging it might be dangerous. She is even doing her post-rapturous smile of edgy resignation. In other words, she is busting out all her standard cutie tricks to make peace, I suppose. Or perhaps it's how she's most comfortable, controlling the level of flirtation and charm. Her face looks angular to me, and tired, and disturbed somehow. Her suggestive lean feels aggressive.

"Look," I say, pointing my chin in the direction of Milan, who's parked himself on a bench at the far periphery, between two hedges. "What's he doing?" I ask.

"He's sitting down."

"He's keeping his eye on things," I say, laughing. "What an idiot."

"He's protective..."

"Look, I accept you love him. Alright? I just don't understand how you can live with all that hand-wringing piety! The self-infatuation. All his Buddhist bullshit! He's no Buddhist. Isn't there some clause about right behavior, something like that? You know he used to tell me sagely, 'You miss emptiness by a hair, you miss it by a thousand miles.' Well, I'll say he missed at least by a hair! He missed by all the big hair in Jersey! He fucks up his family, our life together, his own happiness, and then I'm supposed to feel sorry for his predicament?"

"It's not bullshit, Bob. You know it. He's a real person. These things do matter to him. A lot. Yes, he totally messed up, but he at least saw it, right? He's making change now... And he's very serious about Buddhism. You shouldn't make fun of those things."

"From what little I know, Elena, I know it can't be conducive to enlightenment to abandon your family for some booty-call."

"You are hurt."

"Um, duh."

After some seconds, "You know what I see in him?" She turns to regard him for a moment, staring at us from a distance. "He needs me. He actually does."

"I needed you."

She squints at me, trying to focus. She gets a cigarette and lights it. "No, not really. He needs me to know him. And...

and...you don't operate that way, right?" There is subtle provocation in her voice, but also understanding. I pat her knee like a buddy. "Bob... you staying at Anna's... well... it really upsets Milan. I know you didn't have a choice, but I'm asking you, at least to give us a chance, figure something else out. He's obsessed. It's awful. We can't get past it. So, for me, please..."

I stare at the weasel, now stretching his arms out over the back of the bench and crossing his legs. He checks his watch. "Well, the fact is, I can't even think of moving out now. The good news is there's an offer on the table. But all my cash is tied up. Sub-par liquidity, if you know what I mean? Sorry, baby, I'm stuckaroo."

She looks at her fingernails, her ratty cuticles. "How much money are we talking about?"

"Oh, forget it. I can't take any more money from you. You're already a primary investor."

"Well, then take it as a further investment in Peace INC. You say you got a fish on the line. Alright. When you sell, I expect a great return."

"You'll have it back in months."

"Fine. But, Bob, you'll find another place to live."

I look up at the green patina face of a dancing muse, her mouth half-open in song, her body forever poised in celebration. Her gleeful expression reminds me of Anna last night, a moment when she sat up into a beam of orange street light, and looked down at me. I don't recall ever feeling that kind of sweetness with anyone... "Sure," I say. "Ten grand. I think ten grand should do it."

CHAPTER IX

"You're always scheming, aren't you?" Anna asks. We sit at opposite ends of the couch, and I am shy and awkward. "What's that supposed to mean?"

"Don't get mad. I'm just saying it seems like you never stop hustling."

"I'm like any other animal. No more, no less."

"We're more, aren't we? Or at least different."

I slide a little in her direction, lean to kiss her cheek. "I wasn't hustling last night. I don't think I'm hustling now."

Anna stares at me for what feels like minutes, her gaze weirdly neutral. "I hope not," she says. She gets up, pokes her head into the bedroom where baby Devi is asleep, then quietly shuts the door. She comes directly for me, pushes me down, and unbuttons my shirt. My dream unfolds, but real this time, and I'm not ready. I'm freaked out by the baby in the next room. As her face nears mine, the intensity of her focus makes me retreat for a beat, and our lips barely brush before Anna pulls back too. "I'm sorry," she says, her face red.

"Don't be. I liked it. I was surprised, that's all."

She turns away, and her voice is tiny. "I just wanted to feel something else, you know? Other than the same pain. Sorry."

"Anna, I'm telling you, nothing to be sorry about." I get next to her, smell her sweet neck. "We can do anything we want."

She's very still. "I thought you were a Kashmiri."

"Excuse me?"

"When we first met. You looked like some of my Indian cousins."

"You know them, then? Your cousins?"

"No, not really. I've seen pictures. It's your eyebrows. They look Kashmiri to me."

I'm quiet. She laughs. "The question isn't who you were, Bob, but who are you now?"

"Your friend, I hope."

"Yes. Yes, you are." Her head is tilted to the side, and she's raking her fingers through thick curls. "You know what I've been thinking about? For a while now? How much planning and thinking and scheming it took to bomb those buildings. And how little planning it took for people to help each other... If we truly want peace, we must be peace, right?" She kisses me on the lips and goes to the bathroom, leaving exactly the right amount of time for me to fall properly in love.

Anna and Bob. Bob and Anna. Even our names are made for each other, ready dance partners, happy to twirl in any direction. When it finally happened, our love-making was tentative and ungainly, but also innocent, promising. The passion I feel for her is so different in pitch than what I felt for Elena. (Sometimes Elena was her most attractive and repulsive simultaneously, where the only psychic option she'd leave open was hot boom-boom. Exciting at first, then slowly debilitating.) I can watch Anna for hours on end in a pleasant, light trance. Her every gesture—stirring tea, brushing teeth, working the clickie for the TV, reading to Devi—makes my cells sing. She's strong and gentle, and most importantly, non-judgmental. I want to take care of her, protect her, and the intensity of this primitive drive surprises me. There is some heartache too in yearning for warmth, imagining a family. People get lucky. I'm a person. Why can't I be lucky, too?

The news is grim for the world. All indications are that the theater of war is expanding, though the Terror Channel insists the situation is under control. Blast after blast after blast, this poor earth will have to take it. And we will take it, too. You can see this knowledge in the eyes of passerby, a flicker of buried panic, as they go about partying like normal. I feel it, a deep intimation that civilization is becoming unhinged. Or am I?

It's a warm clear night and even though the moon is nearly full, you can still glimpse a star or two. There's a thronging crowd spilling into the street around the entrance to Fifth World, mostly tattooed and pierced youngsters in tank-tops. I hadn't been to a real night club in many years, but Njal insisted I meet him here, and it was crucial that I come. No paper work is done yet, so his offer on the table could vanish as mysteriously as it arrived.

I never got a sense of how big Njal was and in this zoo, size would at least be a start. Kids scream and shout at the giant bald bouncers with headsets. A steady stream of people make their way inside, each time the door swings open, thumping bass comes spilling out. I circle the crowd, stand to the side, try to push my way in, but there's no sign of Njal. My cell phone rings. "Yeah?"

"Bob?"

"Njal. You'll have to speak up." I plug my ear. "I'm outside. Where are you?"

"Look. We work it out. You see the big bald guy?"

"There are four big bald guys."

"Yah, yah. The big bald black guy. See him now?"

I spot him set back in the sea of nightlife humanity. "I see him."

"Good. Yah, okay. You see a small white hand waving?"

It takes a second, but there's Njal waving. "I see you."

"Okay. Yah. Now, you come this way, understand?"

"I'll try," I say and start pushing my way through again. "Excuse me. Sorry. Pardon me."

"Watch it, asshole," says a vampire goth guy. "Don't push please," says a neo-hippie cutie. I can't see Njal any more, but the big black bald bouncer seems to be moving in my direction. Like Moses parting the Red Sea, the denizens clear a path. "You Bob?" he asks, and before I can nod, he is pushing me through to the entrance, where Njal waits, sporting a rascally smirk. "Alright, Bob," he says, his arms out open to hug. "You made it, yah?"

"Some scene," I say hugging him. Under his striped Mod suit jacket, he's tiny like a child. He makes an impression with his big head and pouty lips. Njal nods to the giant bald man who opens the door. The bass is throbbing as we step into the cool air-conditioning. He leads the way past another set of gate-keepers, leggy girls with short skirts and hard faces, who nod and smile at us. It seems Njal truly is a rock star! We avoid the cavernous main dance floor and wind through a series of dimly lit halls, and turn into a velvety lounge, where pretty kids sip brightly-colored drinks. Njal gets a few casual looks walking to the only reserved table and occupying a spot on the plush red couch.

"Super," I say sitting down next to him. "So, what's up?"

"You should tell me, right? No answer from you guys."

He's worried about us backing out? Superb! "Still discussing, Njal. Talking with our lawyers. But I'm pretty confident we can make it work."

A waitress comes with two tall glasses of seltzer with limes, places them on the table and walks away. "It's a very generous offer we've made. I'm not sure how long we can wait." He stares at me, affectless. "It's not so complicated. Simple yes or no."

"Soon, I promise. But why did we come here?"

"Yah, look. I thought we might have an adventure, okay? What do you say?"

"Depends."

"My god, you see you do it again. Maybe is making everyone miserable. Yes or no, Bob."

"I'm not going to agree to something if I don't know what it is."

"Wise," says Njal, leaning his head back, staring at the ceiling. "But limited, you understand? Timid."

"Big deal."

He turns to me, his eyes half closed. "Yes or no. It all comes down to that, Bob. Yes or no?"

"Sure. Okay, Njal. Yes, dammit. I say yes. Yes!"

Njal perks up and reaches behind the couch and produces two brown packages tied crosswise with red string. He's grinning like a nutcase handing me mine. "Go ahead, open it."

I tear it open and am perplexed to see a Peace INC., T-shirt. Does he know this is like giving a Big Mac to a McDonalds cashier? "Nice shirt," I say smiling in a way that anticipates an explanation. He also has a T-shirt. "So, the reason we have come here tonight, to answer your question, is one DJ from Amsterdam, Abraxas. He plays a little later. See?" He holds the shirt up to his chest and smiles. "There is also this." He places two yellow capsules on the table.

"Whoa. What is that?"

"That is the one they have perfected, understand?"

"Have a name?" I poke at one of the capsules and it rolls toward Njal.

He holds it up to the light for a moment before replacing it next to the other capsule. "Peacehole, man, that is the Peacehole. Yah, they figured it out, these guys. The best part is it's all natural. In a way."

"I don't know, Njal. I don't really do drugs."

"Bob, it's not about the drug, man. Some people who are really solid told me it was worth it. They've made the stuff with some freeze dried pulverized ayahuasca. Something like that."

"You've never done it?"

"No, man. That's what I'm saying. Together. We take the trip and see the land of peace. We say yes and see. Don't you want to see it? If we're going to make this all happen, we have to do it, man. We must find the power, understand? The power place." He picks up the pill and pops it, washing it down with seltzer.

"Njal!" I say, startled.

"You said yes, Bob. Yah, you said it. " I know it is not the provocation which makes my hand mysteriously move to the pill. I know it is not my deep ambivalence about peace itself which drives the pill into my mouth. It's another force I don't understand, a strange optimism, a momentary flash of fearlessness.

Immediately, I regret it. "Alright," says Njal, grinning and slapping my back. I'm considering going to the bathroom and making myself vomit. "Hey, is there some problem?"

"I'm not sure I should have done that," I say. "How long does it last?"

"Bob, man, you must chill out."

"How long?"

"Three, four hours. If we find the peacehole, a few minutes in there. We should go with the right attitude, understand? You want a drink? Might help."

I sip the seltzer, a churning in my stomach. "No, it's okay," I say, but he's already waving to the modelly waitress. "I don't like being out of control."

"Tanquery Martini," says Njal to the waitress, then to me, "Listen, you know very well control is limited. We don't control our birth, man, we don't control our death.

We like to think we make choices, but we don't choose the conditions where we make those choices, understand? It goes on and on, like that, forever, man. Now, we do something totally different. Forget about all that control. We go to the land of peace, man. No control in peace. That is the opposite of peace. Hey!" he shouts to two hotties, who scream in delight and grab each other's shoulders, jumping up and down, before rushing to our table. The churning and gurgling in my stomach worsens and as the hotties smother Njal with kisses my great fear is that I will fart and it will be loud and smelly and terrible.

"Bob," Njal says, "This is Jenny and Jenny." Jenny 1, seated on Njal's lap, offers her hand to shake, and Jenny 2 says "Hi," from the other end of the couch. The two Jennies, tanned, blond, in identical black little dresses, seem like twins in a porno. "Are you related?" I ask.

Njal laughs and kisses Jenny 1 on the neck. Jenny 2 says, "We just met like last year at school, but everyone thinks we're sisters. Plus, we have the same name. "

"Extraordinary," I say, and I am a bit disturbed to realize that though the Jennies are completely legal, they're just kids. "Be right back," I say. I walk over and lean against the bar, sipping my seltzer, watching Njal on the couch, flanked on either side by canoodling Jennies. He sees me and waves for me to return, then starts making twirling motions in the air with his finger. Code for the drug kicking in? I feel nothing unusual, if anything slightly blue and a tinge paranoid in the midst of all these shiny pretty people. Are they all on drugs? *We don't control anything*, says Njal. *Be peace*, says Anna, and the memory of her voice morphs from wise and reassuring to accusatory and glib. How can anyone *be* peace when they are alive? Nothing peaceful about a roiling stomach, a pumping heart, enzymes devouring food, cells in endless war with decay. The life force is always in motion, restless, transforming. If you *are* peace, aren't you dead? Still? Void? The loungy beats are softer now and there are voices mixed, harmonized in octaves like Tuvan throat singers. I watch bubbles cling to the side of my glass, vibrating just enough to push free and float to the top, into air. The whistling sounds barely human, then almost all machine, a low flying jet getting nearer. I blink and there's Njal. "Feel anything?" he asks.

"Little edgy."

Big smile, glittery teeth. "That's it then."

"This is it?"

"Attitude is everything, Bob. Attitude is everything, Bob."

I'm not sure he said it twice. The music is thumpy, the singing Middle Eastern, Egyptian maybe. The Jennies are on either side of him. "We need to borrow him a sec," says Jenny 1, looping his arm. "A sec," says Jenny 2. "Don't move, understand" says Njal. "I'll be right back. I'll be right back."

I nod, my head heavy on my neck, my eyes blinking the room into strobe-lit slices. Passing smiles look ghoulish. Everyone seems dead. Attitude is everything. I attempt a peaceful visualization, a wildflower field, a crystalline stream, a sunny warm day. I look into the water and see a reflection. It's not me, but the boy I was. I see myself, a teenager running, laughing, chasing his friend, chasing a ball. I stop and look up at the electric-blue sky, the mountainous clouds. I see orange bougainvillea shiver in the breeze and an ant carrying a giant leaf. Every blade of grass fully charged. The sky, my best friend. The universe, perfect. I scream and run from sheer exuberance. I run and run and run and run. I play football as mother and father and sister shop for shoes. For school supplies. Far away I hear three blasts and then a few more farther. They sound like fireworks, though I can't remember any festivals. I rush home hungry for dinner, and in the twilight I see my uncle at our gate ready to meet me. There were six car bombs with nails that spray out hundreds of feet. My family was much closer. I wasn't allowed to see their bodies. Dear mother, dear father, my sweet sister… there, then gone. I was there, then gone. Safety, gone. Trust, gone. Hope, gone. Home, gone. Peace, gone. How will I find my way back? And to what? Ordinariness? Obliviousness? The womb? After certain kinds of knowledge, there's no turning back, never. Your only option, Anna says, is to love both good and bad. Engage life with the fewest illusions. Stay interested, regardless. Is that being peace? Truly expecting nothing? How scary is that?

The lounge is suddenly packed, over-perfumed girls and boys pushing me out of the way to order their crayola drinks. I must leave this horrid place. There's a rush in my skull as I stand, and I am steadily propelled through the long halls, taking turns and never reaching anywhere. "There you are," says Njal. "There you are."

"Are you saying things twice?"

He laughs boisterously, throwing his head back. "Yah, just now, I think I did say it twice. Oh ha ha ha ha. Pretty interesting stuff, this stuff, right?"

"I don't feel high or anything."

"Nothing?"

"Maybe like a few cocktails."

"Wow." He meets my gaze, his pupils expanded into infinite caves. "It must have a different effect on people. Because I have no idea, man."

"About what?"

He laughs again. "Exactly." His face is illuminated, angelic. "You remember what we talked about?"

Strangely, I know what he means. "The message of your band."

"Yah. The whole maneuver of Njal's Saga. To go from negative to positive. No to yes. Lead to gold, understand?"

"Positive," I say, and a pattern in the chipped paint behind Njal looks like Anna's profile, her sharp nose, her heart-shaped mouth.

"In Iceland, soon the whole country will run on hydrogen."

"Yes," I say, and I am thinking of holding Anna in bed, waking up next to her for the rest of my life.

"Many things can happen, Bob. We must be open to the possibility of the positive, understand?"

"Njal, I think I have to go."

"But we're going to do this thing, man. DJ Abraxas is just starting."

"It's what you said."

"What I said?"

"About the positive. I see it clearly." Actually I see a faint blue halo around his head.

"The peacehole, man. We're all set."

"Some other time. Sorry. Now, I really have to go home."

"No way, understand? We came this far, man."

"I must go." I tip over against the wall. It's cold on my face.

"Serious, yah? You okay?"

"Maybe I am experiencing a slight effect." My bones feel liquid and cheerful.

He smirks. "Looks like."

"Can you get me out of here?"

"Yah, sure, why not." He leads us through tunnels connecting to other tunnels, past small bars tucked into dimly lit nooks, pockets of swaying dancers, through heavy red curtains, to a back exit. He pushes open the door. "All you need is love, Bob. Love is all you need."

"You're okay, Njal."

He grabs my collars. "Then why not say yes to our damn offer."

Stars everywhere, gliding along the road, high as lampposts, traffic lights, flashing off the pavement. I walk amongst stars. The people passing me are vessels of light, radiant inside, out. If I close my eyes there are clusters and galaxies and nebulae too. I am made of light. The first thing I saw was light, the last thing I will see is light. In between is life, this story written on the light, shaping, giving coherence to infinities of moments. But this so-called meaning is at a price. You pay with radiance.

I knew all this very clearly as a kid, and then lost that knowledge, trying later to create luminosity by an act of will. And now, as Bob separated himself from my so-called past, I feel another separation from Bob. *Not who you were, but who are you now?* My spirit rises slowly above and sees him walking underneath, bewildered, lost. Threads of light connect me to his body and mind, and yet I can see him clearly, objectively. Bob is committed to living in the moment, but he has protected himself from it. The present terrifies him, even more than past or future. The present is a holy terror. To be fully in the moment is to cease to be Bob, or anybody. *Who are you now?* Identity dissolves into pure being, only being. "Nothing to fear, Bob. Nothing to fear," I say. I approach the steps of a shuttered bank, immense Corinthian pillars inviting me to sit. The stone feels cushiony soft, the night air caressing, strollers benign, and my spirit gently descends back to my body, content. The pleasantness reminds me of long ago, of days where nothing had to be done and yet many things happened. Days when the world held me so snuggly that I had no sense of my difference, my isolation. *Who are you?*

College kids in hoodies, a Chinese grandpa, two drag queens in fishnets, a gang of German tourists checking a map, each form is precise and perfect, like grass and trees and daisies. One energy, one intelligence, one consciousness, knowing itself, wildly at play, capable of perfect harmony and unbearable violence. And I am part of this exchange of molecules, a mysterious articulation, subject to all the laws of relationship. Everything decays, everything that is born, dies. All creatures, beings, ideas, notions, beliefs, planets, universes, realizations. Eternity is not a super-abundance of time, but timelessness. Out of time, where *now* is. This most obvious of truths hits me in the chest, and though I struggle to find my breath, I feel lighter, floating and still.

Pages of newspaper blow down the steps. One unfolds next to me with the full page headline : NEW TERROR THREAT. The words break up in my mind into sounds, new terror threat, newterrorthreat, newterrorthreat, new-terrorthreat. I'm not sure why I laugh as hard as I do. The world truly is wretched, but it is, amazingly, the best of all possible worlds. "Yes sir!" I say. It's clear to me now how simple it is to accept life. To know stillness at the center of movement. To be at peace in the midst of disaster. I want to rush home and tell Anna, but even as I start to walk, I'm not sure what I would say. I'm already forgetting what I knew. And the more I think about it, the more agitated I become.

CHAPTER X

She rolls away from me, curling the sheet around her. She mutters and sighs and smacks her lips before resuming the long steady breaths of sleep. Her white-wrapped outline is of a French odalisque, her wild black hair fanning out over the pillow. In the pink dawn light her skin is golden, glowing, her sleeping face calm like a goddess. I kiss her, once, twice, thrice. "Hmmm," she says, grabbing my neck, kissing me back.

"I have to go," I whisper.

"Fifteen minutes." She wraps her arms around me and promptly dozes off again. How can I refuse? Her head resting on my chest, her delicate fingers over my heart? I hold her and smell her and it is paradise. Who's kidding who? I've loved her from the moment I set eyes on her. Milan told me about this great woman he'd met and we all got a cocktail one evening. She was nuts about him, you could see it in her eyes. I was single then, lonely, and although I was genuinely happy for my so-called friend, I also secretly believed that she would be happier with me. Of course, over time, I wrote this feeling off as normal envy and wounded narcissism. I came to love Anna in a platonic way as the wife of my so-called friend. But the first night Anna and I kissed, it was as if a dormant seed in my psyche suddenly blossomed. "Anna, I have to go... now."

"Why?" she asks very much sounding like baby Devi.

"Because I made a promise."

She rolls over again, this time huffy, her back to me. "Your dumb promise. It's not up to him to tell us what we can do." Definitely wide awake.

I slip on my boxers before getting up. I put on my pants, socks, shoes, and T-shirt sitting on the couch. "I promised Elena."

She sits up now, holding the sheet to her chest. "It's not up to her either... You're not really keeping your promise anyway. You've been here four nights this week."

"Yes, but I don't live here. Which was the promise."

Laughing at my casuistry, "That's silly."

"Nonetheless," I say, tying my shoes.

"Why'd you make that dumb promise?"

"Anna, I agree with you. I agree. But until you two settle on custody and rules and who's supposed to and not supposed to see each other and when and what..."

"Yes, yes, yes," she says, covering her face. "I see, I see. Okay. Get out of here." She bops me with a pillow, provoking me to jump off the couch onto the floor for some final rolling around and smooching. "Right," I say finally extricating myself, standing. "Before baby Devi wakes. I'll call you later."

"Bye," she says, "Congratulations." She blows me a kiss as I tiptoe to the door and let myself out silently. She'll lie for another hour with Devi in the bedroom and they'll wake up together. Our great luck, the kid sleeps like a stone. It's too bad I don't get to spend as much time with baby Devi now as I'd like, but I don't want to put her in the position of having to lie about my presence. I show up late, leave early, and occasionally come for an official afternoon visit. Milan found an old Polish woman (a friend of Elena's?) who baby-sits. Apparently the kid likes her a lot, though not as much as me, as baby Devi freely admitted when questioned.

I scurry out in the early morning, frighteningly close to the behavior patterns of the weasel. I catch myself looking around the street for him spying on me. But not even the mirroring and fearful symmetry of our situation can bring me down this morning. The rotting garbage, simmering in the hot night, smells fecund and rioting with life juice. The sidewalks are crowded for so early, the hidden Mexican labor force mobilizing to all radial points.

I look up the street, the steep hill. Late at night I once saw three kids zoom down it on rollerblades, their faces lit like they were truly flying. Now, four Mexicans, evenly spaced, trudge their way up, and though I have studied this hill in its myriad aspects, I have yet to do the most basic thing. I climb slowly, stopping once along the way, and then at the top. I turn uptown to survey the vista of roof-tops and criss-crossed wires and water tanks, smaller brick buildings giving way to colossal projects, the street radiant in the morning light.

I cheer the earth as it circles the sun! The hyper-delicate web of living things! I want to yawp and beat my chest and jump up and down! I want to howl and praise God! Not only because I'm alive (but that too), not only because of beautiful Anna and the love I feel for her (but that too) or the sheer wonder of baby Devi (that definitely, too), but also because it turns out our high-priced lawyer is a god-damn genius!

In the dark ages, any serf knew you needed protection. Those knights may just be gussied-up mercenaries, but you're happy yours is the most badass jouster, swordsman, slayer, whatever, in the land. At least it's comforting to believe it, and Bernie has made a fine showing for himself. He is, improbably, Grace's cousin by marriage, a giant egg of a man, widely feared in Intellectual Property circles. The retainer we offered him, though huge for us, wasn't what convinced him. It was when he saw the "Peace for the Children" video and then contacted his people in the music business for any inside scoop, that he raised his lawyerly eyebrow. Because scoop there was, or buzz, that a video by an Icelandic band was testing through the roof—and most promisingly—for all ages. Baby Devi was a keen litmus: The tykes love it! "Peace for the Children", for the whole family! It's positive, as Njal said. A fierce bidding war was taking place between two music giants for their contract, which had yet to be signed. Further snooping revealed that all the marketing for Njal's Saga was built around our peace sign and website. Yes, with one phone call, Bernie became very interested in our case. He made (by his own admission), an outrageous opening salvo and became even more intrigued when their people didn't dismiss it out of hand. The exchange of faxes and e-mails and telephone calls has been furious since.

I'm waiting for Grace outside Bernie's building in midtown. It's the tail end of lunch break and all the worker bees are rushing back to their hives. Some alone, but many in pairs, groups, chatting, laughing. I want to grab them and shake them and tell them that I've got a *meeting*! And serious *money* is involved! "Hi," says Grace behind me, and I'm surprised to see her in a swanky linen business suit, her hair up, sporting subtle green eye shadow and pale lipstick.

"You don't mess around, chica! Outstanding!"

"Thanks. I thought since we have big meeting..."

"Indeed. You see I decided to wear the Armani."

"Very nice." I lead the way into the building and laugh as we get into the shiny elevator. We get out on the ninth floor and approach the receptionist. "We have an appointment with Mr. Weisman," I say and the prim woman points us to the reception couch. A few minutes later, Bernie comes out to greet us, looking pretty disheveled. He is jacketless, tie loose, and one of his shirttails hangs out of his pants. He lowers his glasses on his nose, giving us the once-over. "You guys already look the part. Great, come on," he says, walking us gingerly through the labyrinth of cubicles into a conference room with a large polished wood table and one of those creepy black ET module speaker phones. "Have a seat, I'll be right back."

"Alrighty," I say and sit in the soft leather chair; Grace examines some antique city maps on the wall. Each moment begins to stretch, movements of people I see through the glass partition, slo-mo; my heart itself sounds slow pounding dully in my ears. On the polished surface of the table I see my faint, distorted reflection, and start to feel woozy, nauseous. Sweat collects on my forehead, my palms, my breath fast now, anticipating calamity. A bomb in the building. A tidal wave just off shore. Flesh-eating epidemic. Grace, uncharacteristically squeezes my shoulder. "Don't worry, Bob. God look after it. God look after us."

I pat her hand, her words oddly comforting. "Sure," I say as she slouches into the chair.

"Okay," Bernie says, coming in with a folder. "First of all, this was excellent fun. I don't know, I thought I'd be dealing with the companies, but, these guys..." He shakes his head... "I don't know what they were thinking. I'd never handle anything this way. See, that's why you're lucky you got me." Sits down, big grin. "Grace doesn't know me too well, but my wife will tell you I have certain ways of doing things." He reaches under the table, and presses a button. A second later the door opens and a clean-cut young man brings in a case of Cristal and sets it on the table. "I'm liking it," I say.

"Yeah, I represented a couple of gangsta-rap guys. You know, sampling problems. They converted me to Cristal from Dom. By the way, that case of bubbly is not from me to you, it's from you to me. Understand?... That's how sweet the number is." He pauses again for pure s/m value. "And the number is... six hundred and fifteen thousand dollars."

"What?!" I say.

"Six hundred and fifteen thousand eight hundred and ten dollars. That's the final settlement. For the whole shebang."

"Oh my," says Grace, covering her mouth with her hand. One of Bernie's conditions taking us on was that we trust him completely with negotiating. He thought it better for everyone if we didn't know. And he's right, because neither of us had a clue it could be that much.

"Holy shit! Bernie! You rule! You totally rule!" I jump up and slap him a serious high five. I run up to Grace, pull her out of her chair and kiss her on the lips. "Six hundred thousand dollars! Holy Moly!" I say, and skip the length of the room. "Six hundred and fifteen thousand dollars! Grace!" I run up to her again, grab her by the shoulders, kiss her face.

She seems to be a bit hysterical, laughing and crying at the same time. "I told you, Bob. If message is right..."

"Absolutely!" I say, dancing around. I skip over and kiss Bernie, who looks like a clean-shaven Santa. "Alright, alright, let's all calm down. Bob, sit down, Grace, please. The sooner we get through this, the sooner we can cut some checks."

I sit, bouncing in my chair, my mind racing ahead to my new life. I want to take Anna and baby Devi to Rome. "Let's do dis, like Brutus, cuz you knew dis..." I say.

"First there's my fifteen percent off the top." He smiles.

"Mais oui!" I say. "Bien sur!"

"And then..." he says flipping through some forms, "There is the ten percent to one Trima printing and another ten percent to one Elena Kozlowski. And all that, it seems, comes out of Peace INC., rather than the parent corporation, Peace LLC..."

"Excuse me?" I say.

"Well," says Bernie, looking up at Grace. "That's smart how you issued all your percentages from a subsidiary company."

"I'm sorry?" I say.

"You remember when we first drew up paperwork?" says Grace.

"Yes?" I say.

"You agreed I get fifty percent, before any money get taken out."

"And?" I say.

"That's part of deal. First in. First out. You agreed, Bob."

"I don't understand." I'm looking to Bernie for clarification.

"It's all pretty clear," says Bernie. "Don't you remember signing these agreements with Grace?"

"Sure, but I didn't think... I didn't know... I didn't... so?"

"Well," says Bernie, "after I take my fee, Grace gets half the money as Peace LLC and then you as Peace INC., split the other half with your investors as per your agreements with them."

"Grace, what is this?"

She is mildly irritated when she says, "Please don't pretend you don't remember, Bob."

Memory is creation, says the Science Section of the Sunday paper. At the moment of recall the mind sifts through near infinities of raw data and strings together a story. And that story is not only determined by what you were paying attention to in the so-called past, but also by the job memory is called upon to do in the present. Memories only occur now. Try to remember an unmemorable day and there will be odd details that jump out. Or try to forget a memorable one and again you will be assaulted by a random texture.

Yes, Grace was correct, of course, it was the agreement we made. I knew she was driving a hard bargain, but at the time I had no choice. Then, conveniently, I did forget. I stayed angry about it for a week or so, until the fattie check came by messenger. Hot damn! I put all grumpiness aside and called her immediately and teased her mercilessly about her number being so much bigger than mine. We made up, no problem.

Trima was extremely pleased with their cut and negotiated with Njal's Saga to stay on as the printer of related material, but they were worried that if it became too huge it would be taken away from them. I told them not to worry, I had other ventures up my sleeve. Naturally, dealing with Elena was more fraught, even though she got a spectacular return on her investment. In the letter I sent with the check, I announced that, ineluctably, Anna and I were now seriously involved. Milan telephoned Anna and was apparently "very upset" about the news. When he came to pick up baby Devi for the weekend, he requested that Anna bring her downstairs because "he didn't feel comfortable" coming to the apartment. Anna and he have been trying to figure out what's best for baby Devi, and Milan tried to make the case that baby Devi becoming attached to me could be very harmful to her psyche when I decided to "pack off." I assured Anna and she assured Milan I had no such plans. Elena and I haven't spoken yet.

When I try to analyze it, I'm not sure exactly why I'm nervous about them coming over. The decision was made between Milan and Anna that for baby Devi's sake, we should all be in a room together when Milan comes to pick her up for the weekend. I admired the courage of the decision, though the last few hours cleaning have been confusing as to the desired effect. Every element of presentation is a puzzle. Is it better if we seem like a solid couple or not?

I remember coming to visit them back in the old days and noticing the new-family chaos in the kitchen. I thought it was charming at the time. But now I realize it was simply a lack of attention. It's not hard to keep a kitchen counter clean, even with an active three-year-old. So now I sponge it down so the Formica shines, and I wonder whether he will take the tidiness as a personal affront. Some insidious chimp posturing. And how to behave with baby Devi? Friendly like normal, or aloof to protect his feelings? I hope she shows him special love as her daddy, I really do.

"Daddy is coming today with Auntie Elena. Yay!" says Anna. Baby Devi doesn't respond, absorbed in flipping the thick cardboard pages of her number book. Hands on hips, Anna stares at her daughter like she's a puzzle. "It'll be fine," I say. Anna turns to me with the same objective gaze, then breaks into a laugh. "What's funny?" I ask.

"I was just going to ask you whether I looked alright." Her laughing gets the better of her for a second. "You know, like we were having a dinner party."

"Yes, it's weird." I walk up and hug her. She's stunning in her Ukrainian peasant dress. "You look much more than alright. Meeeow..."

"Hey, you made a kitty sound," says baby Devi.

"That's right, sweeto," I say swooping down on her and picking her up, holding her high above my head. "Meow,

meow, meow, meow, meow, meow." Baby Devi squirms, laughing like crazy. "Meow, meow, meow, meow," she says as I fly her like an airplane coming in for a landing. "Yay!" she says, hopping around. "Daddy's coming today!"

"I wish they would show up already," mutters Anna, checking the clock.

"They're not even late." On cue, there's a knock on the door. Why didn't they use the buzzer? To prove that he still has keys? Then why not simply use the keys and barge in? Why bother knocking at all? Right, the buzzer doesn't work. I take a cleansing breath as Anna opens the door. Milan enters first, and I must admit he looks good, healthy, vital. Elena tentatively follows and she also looks glowing and yummy in her red summer dress. "Daddy!" yells baby Devi, running up to him to be picked up and held. "How's my bunny?" Milan asks.

"Meow," says baby Devi and perversely that gives me a thrill. I get up from the couch to greet them. Anna, perfectly poised, kisses Milan on the cheek, and says, "Hello," to Elena. "Please. Come in." Anna is so even, you would never guess that this is the first time the wife has set eyes on the mistress. Elena though, has a pained and defensive smile as she says, "Thanks." She doesn't really look at Anna, sitting on the far end of the couch. "Hi," she says to me, timidly.

"Hi," I say back. Milan, holding baby Devi, sits down next to Elena. "So is bunny ready for the beach?" he asks.

"Beach, beach, like a peach," says baby Devi, earning a kiss from her dad.

"Oh, where are you going?" asks Anna.

"East Hampton," Elena sighs in a rich-girl way, as if she is being condemned to the gulag of unfashionableness. "A friend has a time-share on the water." There is a whiff of snobbish apology in her tone. Was she always like this?

"Sounds great," I say. Yes, that's where their robust aura is coming from: They both have serious suntans! I can't stop from imagining them rolling passionately on the beach like in *From Here to Eternity.* I also cannot stop from imagining a satellite-guided bomb zeroing in on the lovers.

"Tea?" Anna asks. Milan and Elena exchange a confused glance. It's clear that Elena wants this over with as soon as possible. "No thanks," Milan says. "We should go soon."

"Have some tea," Anna says. "Elena? Tea?" I can't make out whether Anna noticed Elena's discomfort or not. Whether Anna is (consciously or not) indulging a little revenge.

"Oh... Okay," says the miserable Elena. Milan rests his hand on her sexy tanned thigh.

"Daddy, daddy, daddy, daddy," baby Devi sings like a jingle.

"Bunny, bunny, bunny, bunny," he sings back. I see Anna in my peripheral vision putting the water on the stove, getting the teapot from the cabinet, and then stop near the sink, standing perfectly still, her head down. I'm ready to go check on her when Milan says, "Hey, congratulations on the business, by the way."

"Yes," Elena says, and her smile is familiar and warm. Her eyes for a heartbeat betray an old affection.

"Thanks," I say.

"I saw the video of that band," he says.

"It's getting some play," I say. Anna is moving about again in the kitchen, putting cookies on a plate.

"It's kind of a crazy video," he says. "I mean at the end, where there's Nazi kids, and Commie kids, and Maoist kids, and child soldiers along with girl scouts and marching bands. It's a little creepy for children, don't you think?"

"What can I say? The kids like it. Who knows why? The other song is starting to get some play too. Have you seen it? I think it's called "Peace for the Planet". It's Njal's Saga riding around on Segues. And their surroundings morph from one lush forest to another. Kids like that one too, I hear. As Grace says, it's good for children to think about peace. I mean, the website's flourishing."

"Except now there are all these music promos on it. It's much more commercial." He smiles. "Maybe you sold too early, Bob. Sure looks like more wars coming. It's pretty scary if you ask me."

"Yes," Elena nods gravely.

"You know, Anna and I and baby Devi were in the park the other day and we saw a kid, must have been around twelve, wearing a Njal's Saga T-shirt. And, it was confusing. Because there was our peace sign, and now it means Njal's Saga. But then I thought, no, it also means Njal's Saga, but it still means peace. As Grace says, however the message gets out."

"Well, they're making money. You made money," Milan says. It sounds like an insult.

"Yup," I say, and go to the kitchen. Anna is pouring the hot water into the teapot and I kiss the back of her neck. "How's it going?" I whisper.

"I'll make it," she whispers back. "Grab the tray," she says, and leads the way back to the living room, setting the cups and teapot down. I put the tray on the table and baby Devi says, "Cookies!"

"Just one, bunny," Anna says, as baby Devi grabs three.

"Noooooo," says baby Devi, clutching her chocolate-chip treasure to her chest.

"Listen to Mommy," Milan says... and suddenly the biological family is encased in a bubble. Elena and I smile at each other, recognizing we're currently superfluous. Milan tries to dislodge the cookies from her hands, provoking a loud shriek, "Nooooo." She pushes him away, hopping off the couch.

"Please, bunny," Anna says, reaching out with her hand.

"No!" she says defiantly, but she throws the cookies against the plate, toppling it. She starts to cry.

"Hey," says Milan, wrapping his hand around her belly. Her crying turns into shrieking and she picks up cookies from the tray and throws them on the ground. Anna squats so she's eye-level with baby Devi. "What's going on, sweetie?" she asks, and is answered by a baby slap on the forehead. "Devi!" Anna scolds in her fierce-mother voice. "Enough is enough!" She picks her up and holds her on her hip. Ignoring the peevish resistance, Anna continues to kiss her child's face. "Who's my good girl? Who's Mommy's pride and joy?"

Baby Devi, whose crying was beginning to get routine (in anticipation of the moment when she will forget she's crying), is suddenly swept by a new wave of angst. Though Anna continues to whisper endearments, her sobs again turn to howling. "Shhhhh," says Anna walking them into the bedroom.

Milan watches, leaning slightly forward, with the urge to follow, to be of assistance. His eyes are wide and his mouth is slightly open, like he just finished saying something. He should have gotten up in one fluid motion, because in the moments he hesitates, he will draw more attention to the act. And ho! Elena takes his hand, supportively. He doesn't turn to her, his full attention taken by the slowly quieting baby Devi, by Anna's high singing voice. Finally, the fool disentangles his hand from Elena's and goes into the bedroom.

Elena doesn't let me see her face. She gets up immediately and takes decisive steps out the front door. She doesn't slam it, but does shut it with gusto. The sound makes my stomach jump. Instinctively, I prepare myself for a round of games with Elena, before blissfully realizing that it is no longer my problem. I almost laugh when I see Milan dart out of the bedroom to follow her. She has not gone far, the voices echo in the stairwell, the shouting and pleading (it's hard to make out what's what). I go into the bedroom and baby Devi is on the bed happily gnawing a cookie, Anna next to her, watching. They're pretty together. "What was that?" Anna asks, standing up.

"Oh, theatrics." I wrap my arms around her waist. "Poor Milan."

"Now, now," she says like a schoolmistress.

"You are the best, Anna. I'd do anything for you."

"Even reveal your so-called past, Mr. Bob?" she says into my chest.

I don't deliberate at all when I say, "Sure. Whatever I can dredge up. All yours. Why not?"

"That's nice," she says and kisses my cheek. "But honestly, it's up to you. I don't especially care."

"That was a test?"

"Maybe," she says with a sly smile, her eyes bright. Then the thudding footsteps up the stairs, the door opens, and Milan walks in, a sheepish grin plastered on his face. "She'll just wait downstairs. Sorry," he says, and it sounds completely phony.

I recognize the spell he is under because I have been there myself. The fight resolves passionately, not with a comforting embrace, but rather a tongue-twining, crotch-grabbing, promise of extra-hot boom-boom. And the sublime part is giving over to her shameless manipulation. To feel as if you will be redeemed by her favors. I know all about it. And though he is a defeated man sadly surveying the battlefield, though I must diligently remain calm, at least for the sake of baby Devi, and learn over time to accept and love him, and though he is as sweet as can be as he cradles his daughter, right now I want to stab him in the forehead.

ABOUT THE AUTHOR

Vijay Balakrishnan is a writer and artist living in NYC. He's co-written the feature screenplays *Karma Local* and *Toussaint*, published fiction in Miranda Literary Magazine, and his prose and photographs have appeared in The Paris Review.

10972904R0

Made in the USA
Lexington, KY
03 September 2011